I0522333

THE UNEXPECTED GUEST

A DE BURGH NOVELLA

Deborah Simmons

Publisher's Note: This is a work of fiction. Names, characters, places, and incidents are a product of the author's imagination. Locales and public names are sometimes used for atmospheric purposes. Any resemblance to actual people, living or dead, or to businesses, companies, events, institutions, or locales is completely coincidental.

Published by Bennett Street Books

Book Layout © 2016 BookDesignTemplates.com

Cover Design by Tugboat Design

CHAPTER ONE

His sons were not coming home for Christmas.

Fawke de Burgh, Earl of Campion, stood with his hands clasped behind his back, facing the evidence that swirled before him. Alone in the solar, he had opened the shutters to one of the tall, narrow windows, only to be buffeted by a blast of chill air and its accompanying snow. The weather was worse than in living memory, and he could only shake his head at its fury. Travel during the winter was never easy, but no one would be fool enough to tackle the frozen roads in the week past, marked by a blizzard such as he had never seen. And Campion would not endanger his family simply to indulge a father's whimsy.

Still, he could not deny his disappointment, for he had become accustomed to a yuletide surrounded by his offspring. It was the only time they were all together these days, and Campion had yet to meet one son's wife and see his newest grandchild.

Perhaps the holiday would have been more bearable if so many were not away, but out of his seven sons, only two were here at Campion Castle, the most meager gathering yet. And although he loved them all, the earl knew that Stephen and Reynold were those least likely to cheer him. A clever lad, Stephen had so far squandered his talents in too much wine, while Reynold, cursed with a bad leg, went through life with a grimness that belied all his accomplishments.

With a sigh, the earl shifted, welcoming the bitter wind that reflected his mood. He had never expected all of his sons to stay at Campion, but neither had he thought so many would settle elsewhere. Who would take over when he was gone? His heir was Dunstan, but the eldest de Burgh was busy with his own demesne, in addition to his heiress wife's holdings. Both Geoffrey and Simon had recently taken wives and were content to live in the homes that marriage brought to them. Robin was overseeing one of Dunstan's properties in the south, and Nicholas, eager for new adventures, had joined him there.

Campion was proud of their achievements and their independence, and yet he knew a certain melancholy at their absence. Not only would he miss them, but the holiday itself would not be the same. Such celebrations were the venue of women, as Campion, who had buried two wives, knew well. In the past few years, Dunstan's lady had made sure the hall was decked in greenery and all the traditions observed, but without her, who would see to it?

They had managed to drag the Yule log inside during a break in the weather and, of course, there would be feasting, but who would take the time to make a Christmas bush and insist upon all the games and gifts and songs? Campion pictured himself stepping into the breach, but he could not rouse much enthusiasm for the prospect, especially since Stephen and Reynold would little appreciate his efforts.

The sound of footsteps made him lift his hands to the shutters. It would not do for the earl of Campion to be seen mooning out the window like a dispirited lad. Worse yet, he did not care to have a servant hurrying to shut the cold away from him as if he were enfeebled. Lately, he had noted a certain subtle fussing over him that did not sit well. He might not be as young as he once was, but he was lord here, and he could still hold his own against his knights, if not his brawny boys.

Campion's fingers stilled at the sight of dark movement among the swirling white outside, and he leaned closer, but the snow obscured his vision of the land below. Although it was probably nothing, he would send a man out to check the grounds, he decided, just as the sound of his steward's voice rose behind him.

"My lord! My lord! Ah, there you are! Have you seen them? A small party is at the gate, struggling against the elements."

Not a trick of the eye then, but arrivals in these conditions and so late in the day? It was nearly nightfall. "Let them in,"

Campion said. Closing the shutters, he turned even as he wondered who would be abroad so recklessly. If it were one of his sons, the earl's enthusiasm for the company of family would be tempered by dismay at such a misjudgment. But who else would be about? Certainly no enemy, even one foolish enough to attack the famous stronghold of Campion, would dare the elements, while pilgrims and anyone else with any sense would be inside.

Perhaps a messenger from court, he mused, but such missives were ill news more often than not, and he left the solar with a distinct sense of unease. Still, he knew his duty, and he would welcome any traveler who braved this weather to reach the haven that was his home. He moved down the winding stairs into the great hall, where he gestured for a servant to light additional torches and called for food and lodging for those who soon would enter.

The steward, having delivered his message to a waiting knight, returned. "My lord Reynold has gone to meet them," he noted, and Campion knew that his son would see that those at the gate made it to the hall no matter what the conditions outside. Despite the leg that pained him—or perhaps because of it—Reynold's will was stronger than any of the others.

"Shall I have the hot, spiced wine brought out?" the steward asked, and Campion nodded, tamping down his annoyance at such mundane questions. When Dunstan's wife had lived at the castle, she had served as chatelaine and handled all the details of food and household so well that Campion missed her woman's touch.

In more ways than one, the earl thought, frowning at the thought of the Christmas ahead. Someone would have to place the holly and ivy and bay about the hall in celebration of the season. And although the castle was cleaner than before Marion's tenure, Campion saw that the walls could use a good scrubbing. After Epiphany, he would set the servants to a thorough wash, he decided. Meanwhile, the Yule log burned in welcome in a hall that was spacious and well-appointed, and visitors this night would be grateful for any kind of shelter.

Outside he heard horses, while nearby the murmur of voices rose expectantly. Among them he recognized that of Wilda, one of the female servants, who eyed the entrance anxiously. Always superstitious, Wilda was staring at the doors with great significance, and Campion smiled. Not only did Wilda hold firm to the old belief that the first person to cross the threshold after midnight on New Year's Day was a harbinger of the year ahead, but she thought that those who appeared on Christmas Eve gave an indication of the holiday's happiness.

The arrival of a dark-haired man was thought to be lucky, and since Campion had been blessed with seven such sons, the comings and goings of his own family had provided plenty of omens of good fortune during winters past. Of course, he did not put faith in such nonsense, but his household was more peaceful when the credulous among it were appeased.

And so he watched for Reynold, who was well aware of the servants' expectation, but when the doors were thrust open, it was not his son who was first to step over the threshold. Several people burst inside, shivering and stomping with the cold, and in the lead was a slight figure in a voluminous cape that fell back with a movement to reveal a swish of skirts. No man at all, but a woman, Campion realized, as the servants gasped softly. While they all stood gaping, she flung back her hood, and a mass of black curls spilled out over the green mantle of snow-dusted wool.

"Humph. Well, at least she's got dark hair," Wilda muttered, and Campion swallowed his astonishment to step forward. Although he put no credence in forecasting the festivities based on his guests' coloring, he was as surprised as anyone to find a woman about in such foul weather and on Christmas Eve.

"Father, may I present Lady Warwick, who is seeking shelter from the storm," Reynold said, stepping forward.

"Lady," the earl said with a nod. "I am Campion. Welcome to my home. Please sit down and rest from your journey." A small nod of a pale oval face made Campion push his own heavy chair toward the hearth. She went into it without complaint, and he stood beside, studying the other members of the party.

There was another woman, not dressed as finely, who might be an attendant, several men at arms, and a handful of male servants. No other man was in evidence, and Campion wondered if some disaster marked his absence and the party's presence in his hall. As his own servants took wet cloaks and brought blankets for the group that huddled near the fire, Campion's gaze returned to the dark head by his side.

The mass of hair was rather amazing, for few except young unmarried ladies left theirs down. And even damp, the black curls were such as Campion had never seen before, so thick and rich that he was tempted to reach out and test one fat lock. Stifling the odd urge, he watched the heavy mane slide over one slender shoulder, his attention drawn downward only to arrest itself suddenly, for the lady was removing her boots.

Obviously, they were wet and chilling her, but Campion was momentarily taken aback. Surely, she would rather disrobe in private, and he leaned forward to offer her a chamber in which to do so. But his mouth seemed strangely unable to work as her slender hands tugged at the hose beneath her hem. Campion caught a glimpse of pale skin, the curve of a well-turned ankle and the instep of a small arched foot, before he recovered himself and straightened.

He slanted a quick glance at Wilda's back, glad that the superstitious woman had not seen Lady Warwick's toes, for a barefoot person was not welcome at the yuletide fire, according to some ridiculous belief. Perhaps because the sight was so unnerving, Campion thought, as he sought to regain his composure.

It had been a long time since he had entertained a woman outside of his own family, so perhaps he was out of step with current manners, Campion told himself. Certainly, the circumstances warranted swift action, for the whole party might well be frostbitten. It was his own reaction that bore censure, Campion thought ruefully. He had no excuse for staring or for the slow, seeping warmth that had invaded him at the sight of a little bare flesh. By the rood, he was much too old for such nonsense!

"We have readied a chamber for you, my lady," he said, his voice a hoarse rasp that made him clear his throat. Reluctantly, he peeked at his guest, but she had already tucked her feet beneath her and was taking a cup of spiced wine from a servant.

"Thank you, my lord. I admit that a warm bed would be most welcome." The statement was uttered in a serious tone that held no subtle inflections, so why did it conjure visions of linens heated by his own body? Campion looked away. Perhaps he had been too much in the company of his randy son Stephen of late. And just where was Stephen? Warming a bed, no doubt, and not his own, Campion thought, his lips thinning into a grim line. He had not taught his boys to live like monks, but neither did he approve of Stephen's careless dalliances.

"Thank you for taking us in, my lord," Lady Warwick said, and Campion's attention was drawn to her once more. A woolen blanket had been draped over her shoulders, and she held the wine in both hands to thaw her fingers, pink without the covering of her wet gloves. But she seemed to be feeling better, for she lifted her face and smiled, causing Campion to take in a startled breath at the sight.

She was lovely. The fire suffused her cheeks with life, and now he could see clearly the smoothness of her skin, the thickness of her black lashes, and her eyes. They were a most unusual shade of blue, almost the color of spring violets, and Campion stared again before he caught himself. No wonder his family had begun fussing over him, for only a fool or a dotard would be so dazed by a pretty face. A *young* pretty face.

He returned her glorious smile with a dignified nod. "You are most welcome, of course, but may I ask how came you to be traveling in this foul weather?" *There. Now he had command of himself as he should.*

She drew herself up, and Campion saw a strength that belied her years. Her violet eyes shone with a determination born of possession, of a maturity that made him reassess her age. She was no girl, he realized, but a woman. Still, she was no older than most of his sons. Where was her husband?

"I was on my way to celebrate Christmas with my cousin when we were driven to ground by the storm," she explained. She met his gaze unflinching, as if daring him to pass judgment upon such a foolhardy scheme, but Campion said nothing. He often found it wiser to remain silent while others spoke, and in this instance, his decision was correct, for she soon continued.

"Truth be told, it was not so treacherous when we started," Lady Warwick admitted. Although she was aware of her error, the firm set of her chin told him that she would take no rebuke from him, and Campion felt his lips stir. "We were forced to seek shelter last night at a public inn, and I daresay were plagued with bodily pests for our trouble. We had hoped to reach our destination before Christmas Eve, but, as you can see, we must throw ourselves on your mercy, my lord."

Lady Warwick took no pleasure in seeking assistance, that much was obvious, and Campion had to admire her spirit, although he still had reservations about her single-minded journey. "I am happy to offer a place to stay for you and your company, but what of your husband? Is he waiting with your cousin perhaps?"

At Campion's question, Lady Warwick's expression became positively mutinous. "I am a widow, my lord, and have commanded myself and my household for many years," she said in a haughty tone he suspected was intended to put him in his place. He bit back a smile, for if the most arrogant and fierce of men had failed to subdue him, this stubborn young woman certainly was no threat.

"I see," Campion said, keeping his thoughts to himself. The men in her party moved over to the trestle table to partake of some food, but he motioned for a servant to set her portion upon a nearby stool.

"Thank you," she murmured, a bit stiffly. At his silence, she seemed to relax and setting down her cup, she reached for a portion of cheese. "Your hall is the most beautiful that I have ever seen."

"Ah, but sadly unprepared for the holiday," Campion said. "I fear we lack a woman's touch, and my sons will not be bringing their wives in this foul weather. In truth, I was uncertain what sort of celebrations the season would hold, so your arrival has been most timely."

She looked a question at him as she nibbled daintily.

"Guests will surely enliven what might have been a rather quiet twelve days of festivities," Campion said. Despite her reluctance to seek help, she must see that there was no shame in accepting his hospitality. Travelers were welcomed any time of the year, but most assuredly at Christmas.

Violet eyes widened as she swallowed hard, and Campion leaned forward, concerned that she might choke, but she straightened and held up a hand as if to ward him off. "No. I... Oh, but we cannot stay. I mean, we would not wish to impose upon you for such a time."

"But surely you cannot think to travel in this weather?" Campion asked in surprise. Already, she had admitted the folly of her journey; to attempt it again would make her devoid of common sense.

"Oh, it will probably clear tomorrow."

Campion gave her a jaundiced look, and her gaze slid away from his, making him wonder if there was something to her trip other than what she had revealed. Even if the snow stopped, it already covered the roads, as she well knew. Her speech and bearing marked her as an intelligent woman. Why would she risk her life to pay a visit?

Campion was not a man to pry unless she made her business his own, but if Lady Warwick thought to leave on the morrow, she was mistaken. The stubborn woman was liable to end up frozen to death in a drift, should he accede to her wishes. And no matter how accustomed the lady was to making her own decisions, here at Campion, he ruled.

Still, he had not done so by acting unwisely, and so he kept his own counsel, hoping that after a good night's rest, Lady

Warwick would be better able to see reason. In the meantime, he made her as comfortable as he could, offering her more food, more wine, another blanket...

"Greetings!" The sound of Stephen's voice made Campion glance across the hall. The handsomest of his sons appeared, looking no worse from his apparent frolic except for a slight tousling of his hair. At the sight of the guests, he flashed a smile that could melt the coldest of hearts, and Campion was caught between pride in the boy's charm and dismay at his poor use of it.

"What have we here, Father, visitors upon this Christmas Eve?" Stephen asked, moving closer.

"Lady Warwick, you have met my son Reynold. This is my son, Stephen," Campion said. "Lady Warwick will be staying with us until the weather abates," he explained. To his amusement, she lifted her chin as if to protest, but Stephen stepped toward her and bowed low, demanding her attention.

"My lady. It is indeed a pleasure to be graced with your presence." Stephen's rather smug look suggested he anticipated the usual feminine response to his attractions, but Lady Warwick only nodded in greeting, as if he held little interest for her.

Stephen's dismay at her less than enthusiastic response was almost palpable, and Campion had to curb his smile as he turned to study the lady more thoughtfully. She was an interesting woman—beautiful, intelligent, confident and too discerning to be swayed by Stephen's rather jaded appeal—certainly a rare guest in his household.

Stephen did not give up easily, however, and managed to seat himself on the stool, placing her tray of food on his lap, where she would have to reach for it. Campion frowned. His sons were too old to receive rebukes from their father, and yet, he just might have to speak to Stephen, who seemed to be growing more heedless by the day.

"Have you been traveling far, my lady?" the boy asked, carving a piece of cheese and offering it to her on the point of his own knife. It was very nicely done, but for the drawl in

Stephen's tone that told Campion his son was up to something.

"No, not very far," Lady Warwick said as she gingerly removed the cheese with her dainty fingers. Campion noticed that her answer was oddly evasive. Did she seek to avoid the intimacy Stephen was forcing upon her, or did the question itself disturb her?

"Ah, but how is it then that I have never met you then? Just how close do you make your home?" Although Campion frowned at Stephen's silky sarcasm, he, too, would know more of his guest.

"I live at Mallin Fell, at the manor there."

Campion hid his surprise. That was no simple day's journey even in the best of times, but several days' ride to the east.

"Ah," Stephen said as she nibbled at a portion of cheese. "I am not too familiar with that area and know of no Warwicks there. Who owns the holding?"

The lady bristled. "I do. Now if you will excuse me, my lords, I would see my rest." Eliminating the opportunity for any further questions, she rose to her feet, and Campion had a glimpse of slender ankle as she stood, obviously having forgotten her lack of footwear. But her attendant appeared at her elbow with fresh slippers and she slid them on swiftly.

"Wilda, see Lady Warwick to her chamber, please," Campion said, before Stephen could offer to escort her. The servant mumbled something about females arriving when they shouldn't, but did his bidding, and he watched Lady Warwick move toward the stairs. Although not tall, she held herself so well that her very bearing drew respect. Indeed, she might have been a queen or an abbess or any other powerful woman but for that rich mane of hair. It fell wantonly down her back to her waist and flowed when she walked...

Campion's inappropriate thoughts were interrupted by a snort and a thump as Stephen took the vacated chair with a disgruntled expression. "Haughty wench," he muttered. "She's probably some kind of man hater."

Reynold grunted from his place near the hearth, stretching

his bad leg out before it now that the lady was gone. "Just because she didn't fall into your lap, like every other female?"

Stephen scowled. "If you're so clever, tell me how a young, beautiful widow with a manor and lands, no less, remains unwed?" he asked, lifting a dark brow.

Reynold shrugged, obviously uninterested in such things. "She is not that young."

Campion glanced at his son in surprise, for surely Lady Warwick was not much older than Reynold himself. He again wondered at her age, for Reynold obviously saw the maturity that belied her youthful face.

"Perhaps she is barren," Stephen mused.

"Stephen!" For once, Campion reprimanded his son.

"Well?" Stephen said, sliding him a sullen glance. "What else would keep her from another marriage? Unless she's a shrew, of course, which might be a possibility, considering the set of that pretty little chin."

Campion rose to his feet. He had no intention of watching Stephen sulk because the lady had not swooned over his son in the manner of most others of her gender.

"She's too old for you anyway," Reynold muttered as he rubbed his thigh. The piercing cold outside had probably done little to help it, but Campion knew better than to comment.

Stephen snorted. "She isn't any older than I am. And, anyway, there's nothing wrong with more experienced women. And being a widow, she ought to know exactly what she wants," he added lewdly.

"Apparently, it isn't you," Reynold said.

Choking back a laugh, Campion coughed to cover the noise and headed toward the stairs. Any woman who ignored Stephen promised to enliven the hall, and the earl found himself looking forward to discovering more about the intriguing Lady Warwick. His steps to the great chamber were lighter than before, and he realized, with some surprise, that his heart was more buoyant, too.

Perhaps the Yuletide wouldn't be so dull after all.

CHAPTER TWO

Joy eyed the thin light filtering through the shutters with dismay. Not only had she slept far too long, but the gloom that seeped into the chamber did not bode well for travel. Lying there comfortable and warm in the huge, elaborately carved bed, she felt tempted to stay where she was, to revel in the luxury and relative security of Campion Castle. But she would not trust herself to the hospitality of a man, even one with such a sterling reputation as the earl, and so she rose swiftly, calling for her attendant.

"Roesia, rouse yourself! 'Tis late, and we must be on our way."

"Oh, my lady, must we? I've never slept half so well in my life," Roesia said, stretching slowly. "This place is wonderful!"

Joy could hardly argue. The room was beautiful, furnished with chests and a settle and even some kind of soft carpet to cover the tiles and with a wide hearth to stave away the chill. It was at once both cozy and elegant, and the thought of returning to a frigid ride along frozen roads held no allure. But the need to reach her destination pressed upon her as she reached for her clothing.

"Could you believe the size of the hall and these chambers? Fit for a king! And what about the food that they brought us, even though supper was over? That spiced wine was delicious, and did you try those little tarts with the dusting of sugar?" Roesia asked, sighing with the memory.

"No," Joy said, oddly piqued at her attendant's enthusiasm for Campion. At Mallin, they did not have enough money to buy all the expensive spices that were used in such delicacies, but they ate well enough—simple fare that was probably better for the digestion, Joy thought, righteously.

"And the hot bath, practically waiting for us here in our own chamber!" Roesia added.

"With servants aplenty to bring it," Joy noted, but she had to admit that the gesture had been a thoughtful one, and more than welcome when they were sodden and chilled from their efforts to find shelter. The memory brought her thoughts back to the journey ahead, and she dressed swiftly.

Roesia took her time. "I could grow accustomed to this sort of life," she muttered as she laced up her gown.

"As could anyone, I'm sure," Joy said in a dry tone. The de Burghs were wealthy beyond her imagining. And yet, the castle inhabitants, even those who served, seemed genuinely kind and welcoming. Perhaps it was the Christmas season that moved them to such charity, Joy thought, with a trace of asperity. But whatever the motive, she was not accustomed to charity, and she remained resolved to leave as soon as her train could be readied.

It was with that purpose in mind that Joy made her way down the curved stairway to the great hall, but on the bottom step she halted in surprise at the sight that met her eyes. Last night in the dim light of torches and candles, the vaulted room had been shadowy and huge, but now... Joy drew in a deep breath, for she had never seen anything like it. It was vast and bright and clean, with painted walls and tall windows, with cupboards and settles and chairs and so many trestle tables that Joy blinked in astonishment.

And everywhere, people rushed to and fro, from those dressed in the finest clothing to the lowliest garb. Men and women talked and smiled, their voices creating a constant din, while around them children dashed, laughing and squealing. Servants were busy with flagons, ale flowed, and cups were raised in salute, while the scents of cooking food and spices drifted in from the kitchens.

"What madness is this?" Joy whispered.

Behind her Roesia laughed softly. "'Tis Christmas Day, my lady. Or have you forgotten?"

Joy had forgotten, and she felt an unaccountable sadness at the knowledge. But the celebrations she had known were nothing like this. Although she had always done her best to observe the traditions and provide for those at Mallin Fell, here all was on a grand scale far beyond her meager efforts. There was simply more noise, more people, more food, more laughter and more happiness than Joy had ever imagined. She told herself it was an illusion, a trick wrought by wealth and power, but when she glimpsed her host approaching, the man looked disturbingly real.

Had he been this tall last night? Joy wondered, keeping her place upon the step so she need not crane her neck upward when he reached her side. Had he been this regal, this graceful, this… handsome? Joy swallowed hard as the Earl of Campion dipped his dark head toward her in greeting, his very being emanating authority and strength, yet when he spoke it was with a gentleness that she felt right down to her bones.

"My lady, may I wish you a good Christmas and bid you join our celebration," he said, smiling pleasantly.

"Thank you," Joy said, her mind vainly groping for a more intelligent reply. The earl's gaze held her, and for a moment she had the absurd notion that he could see right inside her. The idea brought her wayward thoughts back to her purpose, and she lifted her chin, determined to politely refuse his welcome and be on her way.

When set upon an objective, Joy usually was formidable, despite her dainty frame. Indeed, Roesia often said that when determined, her mistress was an irresistible force. However, neither one of them could have anticipated the earl, who, for all his cultured manners, looked to be an immovable object.

He simply would not budge, Joy realized as he led her to a chair at the great table, yet he did so in a quiet, elegant way that disguised his high-handedness so well that another woman might not have recognized it. Although Joy was not deceived, she was forced to admit that she liked his style. No matter what she said, Campion smiled and nodded, as if in agreement with her, but then he insisted that she stay for the feast.

She told him that she must go, but he would not hear of it,

and he turned aside her every protest with a graciousness that was neither bullying nor condescending. As they argued in a most civilized manner, Joy wondered if the earl ever lost his temper or if he even possessed one, for he seemed to be the most composed of men. He would make a formidable enemy, she suspected, and the knowledge made her reluctant to continue her protest.

Even as Joy reconsidered her position, it became apparent that the meal was about to begin, and she knew she would be churlish to delay it with her departure. Eyeing the faces of Roesia and her men, only too eager for fine food and some holiday cheer, Joy found she could not refuse them. With a lift of her chin, she nodded to Campion, poised despite her capitulation.

"Very well, but only for the feast. Then we must go," she said. Campion's answering smile was nothing more than a courtesy, yet Joy felt a warmth that she could not explain, as if he were truly pleased by her presence. She told herself it was nonsense, but she could not deny that the earl had a way about him that was very appealing. His paternal air was deceiving, Joy realized, as she studied him more closely, for he was not old. Indeed, he was still young and vigorous, and there was something about him that she found attractive.

Smiling at such foolishness, Joy shook her head, but her gaze followed Campion as he rose to announce the beginning of the feast and to introduce his guests. Joy stood and murmured some pleasantries, but she could not help feeling a little awed as she looked down the long line of trestle tables filled with castle residents, knights, servants, villeins, and freemen from the vast lands of the de Burghs. A great, deafening shout rang out as they raised their cups, and then the boar's head, the traditional Christmas delicacy, was carried in to much fanfare.

Roesia's words echoed in her head. *I could grow accustomed to this.* Although Joy had never paid much attention to food, she could not ignore the taste, the variety, and the sheer size of the courses. There were more than the twelve special dishes called for by the holiday, as platters of beef, mutton, turkey, and cheeses were accompanied by sauces, mustard, apples, and nuts, and followed by frumenty, posset, mince pie, and pudding.

While she ate, Joy studied the great hall and its inhabitants. The household was predominantly male, and when Campion spoke to her of his seven sons, she was not surprised. There was no chatelaine and no ladies in waiting. The few women who sat at the lower tables appeared to be wives of the many knights, while farther down there were those who were villeins or married to farmers.

Joy sat on the earl's right, but found herself sharing a trencher with his son Stephen. A more typical example of his gender, Stephen was spoiled and arrogant, and but for the looks they shared, she would hardly think him Campion's son. The other son in residence also was little like his father in demeanor. He was quiet and rather bitter looking. Foolish boy, Joy thought, as she saw all that he had before him. He should be thankful for his lot instead of ruing a slight limp, but wasn't that just like a man?

Lost in her thoughts, Joy was startled when Stephen leaned close, brushing against her breast as he cut her meat. "Thank you, but I can do that myself," she said, putting him in his place with cool smile. Although he moved back an appropriate distance, the boy sulked for most of the meal, drank too much wine, and then began taunting his brother. Joy felt like smacking him on the head and ordering him to behave, the spoiled churl.

Finally, he took an interest in her attendant, and though Joy would not wish such a fellow on Roesia, she enjoyed the respite. Peace and prosperity. It was evident in every filled cup and in each voice raised in speech or song between the courses that filled the groaning tables. There was no desperation here, no worries over harvest or money or allegiances, Joy noted with a twinge of envy.

And yet, none of the revelers misbehaved. The loud voices never erupted in anger or drunken debauchery, for Campion set the tone for the hall. He was the calm, solid center of it all, radiating a power and strength that few men could wield on the battlefield, let alone seated in a chair at the head of a feast table. Joy had always disdained men of rank as bullies, but here was a true lord, a man who ruled through wisdom, not force.

Looking around her at the happy faces and then back at the man who reigned over all, Joy knew a brief yearning to be a part of this place and its people. She had always thought of the de Burghs as mighty knights, but now she began to wonder if she were not seeing the real family now. It encompassed all of the earl's subjects, drawn together here in a realm of his making, where honor and goodness reigned.

Perhaps she had partaken of too much spiced wine, Joy thought ruefully, or more likely, too much of the Christmas spirit. It pervaded the hall in a way that made her think such warmth was present year-round, when she knew that no home could be as wonderful as Campion Castle appeared to the eyes of an outsider. Visiting here was like a trip to some fantastic land of plenty, but as pleasant as it might be, her brief sojourn had to come to an end. And soon.

Despite the temptations of the Yule hearth and friendly people, the promise of singing and other celebrations that would drag the feasting on most of the day, Joy felt the press of time, urging her to be gone. And so she leaned close to Campion's chair, a finely carved oak piece that she recognized as her seat of the night before. He had given her his chair, she realized, swallowing an odd lump in her throat at the gesture.

"My lord," she began, but he cut her off with a smile.

"Campion. Please call me Campion."

"Campion, I would thank you for this wonderful meal, but we must be on our way," Joy said firmly. Instead of dismissing her with a wave of his hand, as she expected, the earl bent toward her. He probably did so in order to be heard above the noise, but he was so near that Joy could see the strands of silver in his hair and the fine lines that fanned out from his eyes on his sun-darkened face.

And what beautiful eyes, Joy marveled. They were not as

dark as she had first thought, but a light, clear brown that seemed to hold the wisdom of the ages in their depths. Joy felt herself drifting toward them, as if drawn by what she might find there—mysteries, truths, peace, and something unknown. A blush rose in her cheeks as she jerked backward suddenly, aware of a strange, unsettling sensation.

Campion appeared not to notice. "Surely, my home is not so lacking in Christmas welcome that you would refuse my hospitality?" he asked. Joy took a shallow breath and shifted warily as she tried to recapture her concentration. She had never learned the subtle game of convincing an arrogant man that her will was his idea. Indeed, she had been accused often enough of being unnaturally forceful, of not knowing her place, and worse.

"Nay, my lord, but I have dallied too much already at your fine table and must hurry to my destination." Joy forced a smile that she hoped was cajoling, but too many years as her own mistress probably made it more intimidating than anything else.

Campion studied her silently, and if he had been any other man, Joy might have known a twinge of fear. One could never be too careful with the volatile members of the opposite gender, to whom an unprotected woman was often fair game in terms of property, money, or desire. But it was hard to impute Campion with such motives. Indeed, he was the first man Joy had ever met who seemed wholly comfortable with himself. He had lands, wealth, and power aplenty, and the very thought of the calm, collected earl suddenly succumbing to urges of the flesh was nearly laughable.

So why wasn't she laughing? Instead, Joy felt an odd sort of warmth at the very notion. Campion's head was tilted toward her slightly, his attention almost a tangible thing, such was the intensity of his regard. And Joy suppressed the impulse to squirm underneath the direct gaze of those enigmatic eyes.

"I understand your wish for a swift journey, but I fear that you will make little progress in this weather," the earl finally said. "I'm sure you do not want to repeat your experience of last evening, yet the conditions are little better today, for the villeins and freemen who journeyed only as far as their own farms this morning were full of stories of the fierce elements."

It was no rebuke, but a gentle reminder, and Joy frowned. A glance toward the tall narrow windows showed the light was still thin and pale, a sign that the sky had not cleared, and she knew that yesterday's drifts had been nearly impassable. The need to be off, and soon, warred against the temptation to linger here in the stronghold Campion had carved for himself, an island in a stormy sea of troubles, where the world didn't seem to intrude.

But Joy had never been one to hide from her duties or lean upon a man, even one as elegant and powerful as Campion. She lifted her chin, resolved to depart, yet even as she would speak, the earl leaned toward her once more, as if imparting wisdom for her ears alone.

"Forgive me for speaking plainly, Lady, but in this weather, you are more likely to die upon the road than reach your destination," he said.

Joy opened her mouth to protest, but at his somber look, so fraught with reason, she thought better of her speech. He was right, of course. She had let her fierce determination cloud her judgment.

Joy looked around the hall, at Roesia flirting with the earl's son, at her men talking so easily with the knights of the castle, drinking their ale in warmth and comfort, and she felt a villain. Should she order them out, they would loyally do her bidding even to their death, and, as Campion reminded her, that was a distinct possibility. All too well, she remembered the blinding snow and the fear that they might not reach shelter before the horses reached the limits of their endurance.

Only a fool would dare such forces again, Joy thought, ruefully. Although no fool, she was so accustomed to taking charge and so intent upon her goal that she had been blinded to all else.

"Lady." Campion's low voice startled her, for Joy had nearly forgotten his presence. When she turned toward him, she wondered how that had ever happened, for her senses hummed with awareness at his nearness.

"I cannot let you leave in such conditions," he said. His expression was gentle yet implacable, and Joy bristled. Did he truly think to stop her? "Tell me why you must hurry, and I will do my best to help you in any way I can," he added softly.

Joy glanced away from his probing gaze. "I wish only to be in familiar surroundings during the Yuletide. And although your offer is very gracious, let me assure you that I have taken care of myself for many years."

"Obviously," Campion answered, his lips curving slightly, and Joy found her outrage seeping away. It was hard to remain angry with a man who had a sense of humor, especially when he was in the right. Joy had always thought males the more stupid of the genders, no matter what the church's doctrine on the subject, for it was usually men who fought each other, who were ruled by their lusts for power and such.

Yet she could not imagine the earl of Campion being ruled by anything. Here was a man to admire and even emulate, Joy decided, coveting some of his calm composure. For years, she had done her best to maintain her holding, making informed decisions with a clear head, but she knew there was a part of her nature that was given over to impatience and argument, which she did her best to subdue.

She saw no such imperfections in Campion. Indeed, it was difficult to find any fault with the earl. Although Joy never had taken much note of a man's appearance, she could not deny that she found him handsome. His face was narrow, but strong, his dark hair sleek, and the streaks of silver in it only added to his innate dignity. Yet it was obvious he was a knight, for lean muscles were evident beneath the fine fabric of his tunic. Joy's gaze lingered along his broad chest before skidding away.

"Very well. I will accept your generous hospitality for another night," she murmured, trying to rein in her unusual thoughts.

"Not another night. You must stay for the entire Yuletide," Campion said. When Joy glanced at him in alarm, she found his manner serene, not threatening. "I have already told you of my sons and their families and how the weather has prevented them from joining us this Christmas. And since these same conditions have conspired to bring you to Campion, I charge you with staying in their place and bringing joy."

Joy stared at him in surprise. "How did you know?" she asked, wondering if the earl was omnipotent, if his eyes could truly see another's soul and the secrets hidden there. Or had he some knowledge of her of which she was unaware?

"Know what?" he asked, his expression puzzled.

"My name. My name is Joy."

"How lovely, but I knew it not," he said, in a charming, yet genuine manner that chased away her momentary fears. "I meant only that we wish for visitors at this time of year, to add to our happiness." His smile was oddly wistful, and Joy was rocked by a sudden, sharp realization.

He was lonely.

She looked about her at the vast hall, filled with people, at Campion's sons and knights and servants and villeins, and she wondered how the man could want for anything. Yet he did. She knew it as surely as he now knew her name, and the knowledge made this man not omnipotent, but oddly human. And it was that glimpse of vulnerability that swayed her far more than warnings of foul weather ever could.

Joy glanced back at Campion, at the polite smile that curved his lips, and she wanted to ask him outright if he missed his family. But would the earl, so dignified and poised as he faced her, admit to such a frailty? Joy doubted it, and somehow she found his elegant veneer frustrating, as if that tiny peek had whetted her appetite for the true Campion. She let herself meet his gaze and wished that she could see behind those enigmatic eyes to the man who dwelled within.

"I will remain only if you let me do something in return for your generosity," Joy said. "You have complained of the lack of greenery and such Christmas trappings. You must let us hang some bundles upon the walls and help to organize the feast, as your son's wife would do, were she here."

"If you wish, but I will hold you to no such bargain," the earl said. "You shall do only as much as you will and take the place of Marion only when you are inclined."

Although Joy nodded, she felt oddly discomposed, as if all between them was not settled to her satisfaction. Perhaps Campion's slow, confident smile was to blame, for it told her he had harbored no doubts about his powers of persuasion. Or perhaps she was dismayed by her own impulsive agreement, a decision based more upon emotion than logic.

But Joy suspected her discomfiture had more to do with the earl's final words, for she wanted to be considered his equal, not a relative. And, although she could not have said why, she especially did not want to be mistaken for his daughter.

CHAPTER THREE

The day after Christmas dawned bright and clear, much to Campion's disappointment. After the gloom of recent weeks, he should have been glad to greet the sunshine, but his thoughts immediately turned to his guest and their bargain. Would she remain to honor it? His instincts told him she was a woman of her word, but he sensed, too, that she was not telling him everything.

What did it matter, if she stayed or went? Campion chided himself, and yet he could not deny a particular fascination with the beautiful Lady Warwick. She was intelligent and competent, no simpering maiden, but a forthright woman with opinions on every subject. He smiled as he recalled the lively debate she had brought to his tired hall during the long day of feasting.

The place was looking a bit livelier, too, for she had already hung some greenery, tied with brightly colored cloth over the doors, and had promised more. He chuckled at the memory of how she had bedeviled his sons until they had braved the snow to gather branches for her. Stephen had grumbled and called her the Christmas Commander, but Campion had admired the way she took charge without being loud or brash. He could well use her firm, but gentle aid year-round.

The thought gave him pause. Ever since Marion left he had missed a woman's fine hand, the presence of a chatelaine who would make her own decisions without deferring to him. Idly, Campion wished that he could convince the capable Lady Warwick to tarry after Epiphany, but she had a journey ahead that she had already interrupted and her own manor to attend. Why would she forsake it for Campion? And she could hardly remain at the castle indefinitely unless she joined the family, he mused, but the idea of her marrying Stephen or Reynold somehow made him uneasy.

His mood suddenly soured, Campion listened to a servant's report upon the dairy and the extra butchering required for the holiday, but his thoughts were elsewhere and he finally dismissed the fellow with an absent wave before hurrying toward the hall. He realized, even as he made his way down the stairs, that the anticipation seizing him exceeded what was warranted by the presence of guests.

His relief, too, was excessive, but it rushed through him, nonetheless, when he saw her. She was seated in the massive chair next to his own, as if she belonged there, and Campion knew a distinct sense of satisfaction at the sight. Even Reynold, looking more grim than usual when leaving the hall, could do little to disturb his odd feeling of contentment.

"Hail, Father!" Stephen said with a courtly bow, and Campion wondered, not for the first time, how his wayward son could carouse all night and then rise in the morning, looking no worse for it. "We're going skating," Stephen said, lifting aloft a set of sharpened animal bones.

Campion saw that several knights and a few of their ladies were already donning their cloaks, and he knew that the weather would be perfect, crisp and clear after the recent temperatures, which ought to have turned the pond that lay outside the castle walls into a heavy sheet of ice.

"But I cannot convince our lovely guest to try the sport," Stephen said. Turning toward Lady Warwick, he bowed again. "I fear she is reluctant to trust herself into my care, but I will not let you fall, my lady. Come," he said in his most persuasive tone. Although Joy shook her head firmly, Stephen pressed her, leaning close until Campion stepped forward.

"Perhaps I shall join you," he said. Stephen swiveled toward him to stare in surprise, and Campion could see the question in his son's gaze. It did not reach his lips, however, for Lady Warwick's attendant took the opportunity to seize Stephen's arm.

"I would be most grateful, if you would teach me, my lord," she said, flashing him a smile, and Stephen's momentary dismay was lost in an answering grin.

"Of course, Mistress, I would be happy to teach you everything I know," he said, and Campion shook his head as he watched them go. Although people were already crowding the hall, the earl found himself alone with Lady Warwick at the head of the high table, and he fought back the urge to apologize for his son. Stephen was old enough to handle himself, even if his behavior had veered wildly of late.

"Do not tell me that you really intend to strap these outrageous things to your boots!"

Campion turned his head to see Lady Warwick with an amusing expression of distaste upon her lovely features as she fingered the narrow bones. His attention caught, he smiled down at her. "Yes," he said, and the word hung in the air in a manner that forced him to clear his throat. "I learned to skate when I was just a boy."

"But, why?" she asked. Her dark brows knitted together as if she were truly bewildered, and Campion laughed.

"For the simple pleasure of it," he said, his mind drifting against his will to other pleasures that he had been too long without.

Lady Warwick looked dubious, still, and he reached out to take her hand. "Come, I will show you," he said, leaning over her. It was a simple gesture, an innocent one, but the feel of her small fingers in his own was enticing, and when his gaze met hers, he felt a moment's disorientation, just as though those violet eyes were calling him home.

It was over too swiftly for Campion to pursue that line of thought, for she tugged her hand from his with an awkward air of confusion. "I don't think so. I am not one for games or frivolous activities."

Campion wondered just what she considered frivolous. She looked so serious, her dark head bent, her hands in her lap, that he frowned. Had she lost her sense of fun with her husband's death, or had she never been given the chance to cultivate it? Either way, he was determined to gift her with an hour of play.

"It is not dangerous. You need not fear injury," he said.

As expected, her chin lifted. "I am not afraid of hurting myself."

"Then, come," Campion said, straightening. His words were a challenge, and as he suspected, Lady Warwick could not resist. A twitch of her lips told him that she was well aware of his tactics, but then a slow smile spread across her face that nearly knocked the wind from him. Joy was not merely lovely, she was breathtaking, and Campion stood staring at her for one stunned moment.

"Very well," she said, rising to her feet, and Campion found himself considering her late husband. Had the man appreciated his bounty, or had he been too often away to entertain his young wife? Had he been a man of intelligence who thrived on his wife's wit or an oaf who condemned her as stubborn and willful? Campion always had been interested in people, and he told himself that therein lay his curiosity even as he suspected he was becoming far too fascinated by Lady Warwick.

After they had donned their gloves and cloaks, Campion led his guest through the great doors of the hall into the bailey and took a deep draught of the crisp air. Beside him, Lady Warwick eyed the brewery and various buildings with approval, and Campion felt an intense pride in his demesne that he had not known in a long time. Indeed, he felt better than he had in years as they followed the path of trampled snow, and when they reached the pond, he stopped to admire the scene, made singular by the winter's unusual amount of snow.

Around them, the world was covered in white, fluffy mounds that curved over a hillock and topped the gnarled oaks whose branches dipped beneath the heavy burden. And ahead lay the pond, shimmering in the sunshine, yet solid as stone, for upon it several of those from the castle skated, along with some of the freemen from the village.

His land, his people, Campion thought, with a certain happiness. And beside him, his unexpected guest. He turned to see that Lady Warwick had thrown back her hood, revealing the thick black curls that fairly gleamed in the light. Her cheeks were colored with cold, her lips curved into a gentle smile that echoed his own awe, and Campion savored the joy of the moment, of pleasure shared and anticipated. He urged her over to a large rock, where they donned their skates, but the rest of the group was too boisterous, so he led her to a more secluded area of the pond, where dark branches hung close to the frozen water.

Considering that he could not remember the last time the pond had frozen, let alone when he had skated its surface, Campion was surprised at the ease with which the skill returned. Sweeping ahead in a long curve, he returned to halt before his student and held out his hands. Although she gripped them, her initial steps were unsteady, so Campion slid an arm around her as he drew her onto the surface, keeping a solid stance while she struggled to find her balance.

As he moved forward, taking her with him, Lady Warwick swayed precariously, flinging an arm around his waist to grip him tightly. Campion took his time, adjusting himself to her tentative efforts as he began a gentle arch across the ice. They proceeded slowly, while he murmured advice and encouragement until, at last, his companion seemed to be able to stand without difficulty.

"Why would anyone want to do this?" she asked. Yet she followed the question with a laugh, and Campion could see she was enjoying herself. Skating might be a foolish pleasure, but life was too short not to make the most of each and every one of them, and Campion was glad to serve as her teacher. As she gained confidence, he took them farther across the water, gliding smoothly for a long moment before he glanced down at her face.

That was his mistake, for the look of wonder there nearly took his breath away. Her violet eyes glittered above pink cheeks and pale skin, her delicate mouth was drawn wide in a white smile, and gazing at her, Campion faltered. She shrieked and they swung around, grasping wildly at each other before regaining their balance as they laughed.

They were facing each other now, hanging on to each other's arms, and a sudden sway of Lady Warwick's body made Campion bend his head near. Suddenly, he was aware of the scent of her, womanly and inviting. His lips brushed against a thick lock of her hair, and the sleek softness affected him in more places than he cared to admit.

With a low grunt of dismay, Campion gingerly set her away from him. They had been too close, and he put some space between them, sliding his hands down to hold her own. She was becoming more adept now, and he glided backward as she followed him forward. In this manner, they circled their small area of the pond, hidden by the curve of the bank and the drape of the snowy trees, until Lady Warwick was wreathed in smiles.

"See how well you skate!" Campion said. "You like it."

"Yes, I like it," she said, in a low, breathless voice that made him clear his throat. He let go of her hands, and she squeaked in protest, but continued on her own.

"Look!" she cried, obviously delighted with her new skill, and Campion watched in admiration as she gained speed, moving into a long curve. He thought of the women he had known since he had buried his wives, fancy ladies of the court who were interested in money and power but not in a rowdy family of growing boys, women only too eager to pursue a wealthy widower, but far too elegant to dash about on a frozen pond.

Lady Warwick was different. If she enjoyed this, then wait until the flowers were in bloom and... he drew up short. Joy wouldn't be here come the spring, he realized, and he felt the slow seep of disappointment into his bones. His smile faltered, and he glanced away at the white hillside where Campion rose, its golden towers no longer as bright as they once were, the haven it provided somehow lacking.

"Oh! But how do I stop?" Lady Warwick's shriek brought Campion's attention back to her, but it was too late. Her eyes wide, she was heading straight for him, arms flailing, and even though he reached out to slow her, she knocked him off his feet. He fell backward, and they both landed in a heap on the ice, laughing as they struggled to sit upright.

"Are you hurt?" Campion asked, relieved when she shook her head in response. Despite their spill, he had never felt better, for this little jaunt had him pulsing with life. But it was not only the skating that affected him.

Joy was on his lap, beautiful and young and full of energy that seemed to feed his own, and suddenly, he was assaulted by images and urges better suited to his randy son Stephen. He felt in the grip of something inexplicable, as if possessed, and to his horror, the pressure of her small derriere on his lap made him hard, painfully so.

Campion's hands shook as he lifted them to her face, and he wanted nothing more than to bury his fingers in her heavy hair, to draw her close, to kiss her lips and more... to slake this frantic thirst with her body. He dared a glance at her eyes, expected to see a reflection of his own shock, but instead she simply stared back at him, violet depths wide and precious as gems. The world stilled, the air around them so hushed Campion could hear her breath and feel its warmth against his skin, as temptation warred with honor within him.

A shout from across the pond made them both start, and grateful for the distraction, Campion rose, sliding her from his lap and helping her to her feet. His hands fell away, and he didn't know whether to laugh at his own folly or apologize. He could not recall a situation so awkward, but then he could not recall ever being in the grip of so fierce a desire.

Desire.

Joy blinked, drawing her trembling fingers back to her sides as she tried to regain her lost composure. For a moment she had been struck motionless by a blossoming heat that could surely melt the ice beneath her. And it had been so sudden, so unexpected that she had not even recognized the sensation for what it was.

Desire.

She had always scoffed at ladies who sought liaisons with men, for they did little to refute the Church's claim that women were ruled by their lusts. As a clearheaded female capable of managing her own affairs, Joy had held herself above such nonsense. She admired a handsome form as well as the next woman, but she had never been prompted to act upon such admiration. *Until now.*

Joy shivered at the thought of her position upon the earl's lap, her initial laughter fading in the face of his warmth. She had felt the strength of his power, of a protection such as she had never known, and then the slow curl of awareness, of his nearness. Her heart skittered, and she rubbed her arms as if to ward off the unusual reaction.

"Are you cold? Let us return to the castle," Campion said, looking maddeningly unaffected by their near embrace. Perhaps she had imagined the excitement in his enigmatic gaze, for now he evidenced nothing more than a polite interest in her welfare.

Joy nodded, eager to take a respite from the earl's heady company, and she moved shakily toward the bank as she sought an explanation for her peculiar response to him. Campion was just a man, she told herself. He walked and talked like any other... except that his voice was so deep and husky that it managed to both sooth and rouse her, and he moved with an appealing grace possessed by no other, whether gliding over the frozen pond like something out of a dream or striding across his hall.

Joy swallowed hard, wondering why this man, among all of his gender, should affect her so. Of course, he was handsome. All the de Burghs were accounted dashing and good-looking, though Joy had not been particularly impressed by the attributes of Stephen and Reynold. They could not hold a candle to their father.

But it was more than his pleasing countenance that attracted her. Joy considered that as she sat down to remove her skates. The straps were tangled, and she struggled with the wet leather until a pair of hands pushed her own aside. Campion knelt before her, and Joy's eyes widened as she stared at his dark head. His fingers, without their gloves, were as elegant, yet forceful, as the rest of him, and Joy felt a renewed warmth at his touch. When his palm slid up to cup her ankle in an intimate hold, her whole body blazed in reaction.

Perhaps it was the way he carried himself, Joy thought, as he made short work of removing her skates. Power sat upon his shoulders so easily, as if nothing could shake his quiet strength, and yet he was not arrogant. It was a confidence born of honor and of knowledge, she decided, as he helped her to her feet.

Joy had often condemned members of the male gender as fools, but Campion was truly intelligent, with a mind open to differing opinions. Not only did he have a great store of book learning, along with his vast life experiences, but he possessed some kind of innate wisdom that shone in his eyes, which Joy found extremely provocative.

All that was very fine and cerebral, but how to explain the jolt of awareness she knew at his nearness, the rush of heat to parts of her that had never known any warmth? Joy felt the loss of his touch like a tangible thing as he moved beside her to walk the snowy path. She shivered again, for as much as she wished to shrug away those sensations or deny them, Joy had always been truthful with herself. And the truth was that for the first time in her life she wanted a man.

Joy was so startled by the admission that she halted in her tracks, staring blindly at the broad back of the male in question. The very notion of her being seized by overwrought desires ought to have been horrifying, shocking at the very least, but instead of gasping, Joy choked back a laugh. For what could possibly come of her wanton yearning?

Of all the men in the land she had surely chosen the only one who possessed far too much honor to succumb to passions of the flesh.

All through the feast, Joy watched him, trying to discover why, Campion, of all people, should suddenly provoke her heretofore nonexistent ardor. But by the meal's end, she was no closer to answers than she had been when sitting in his lap upon the ice.

The want was just *there,* thrumming in her blood whenever she looked at him, and when she did not, it grew more insistent, like an unsatisfied craving. Never before had a man aroused such interest in her, and being of a curious nature, Joy was driven to closer scrutiny.

And the more she studied him, the more interested she became. Everything about him became noteworthy: the way the strands of silver streaked his dark hair, the way his dark green tunic fell across his broad chest, the width of shoulders that were imposing and yet not intimidating. Campion was not a man to wield his power recklessly, and that knowledge was almost as exciting to Joy as his physical form.

Her gaze dipped to his graceful wrists and long, slender fingers, and she flushed with heat as she remembered the feel of them over her own. Strong. Protective. Exciting. How could the sight of a man's hands, regal in repose, thrill her so? It was absurd, and yet, undeniable. This incredible new feeling had seized her just as surely as the Christmas spirit had hold of all else in Campion's hall.

In fact, Joy might have thought her desire some kind of strange consequence of the season or her luxurious surroundings, but she knew no such thrill when she looked upon Reynold or Stephen or any other man present. It was only Campion who affected her so. Of course, she rarely met men of the earl's rank, but those she had known had annoyed her, more often than not. Not so Campion.

Joy felt giddy as a young girl, as the young girl she had never been, while she sneaked peeks at his elegant countenance. In the space of two days time, it had become familiar to her, achingly so, like a favorite treasure one could not bear to put away.

Even as she looked on, a child approached the earl's massive chair as if to speak with him, and Joy held her breath. But unlike most of his sex, Campion did not rebuff the youngster.

He leaned forward to answer her with a gentle smile that filled Joy with heat and song, as if the celebration around her echoed in her very being.

Not for the first time, she realized that when Campion gave someone his attention, he gave it full measure. He did not fiddle with his cup or glance away or evidence impatience of any sort. The earl did nothing idly, but focused himself wholly upon his audience, large or small, man or woman. And when that powerful regard was turned toward her, Joy felt as if she was the center of his world, the single most important person alive.

It was silly, of course, and at first, Joy had found the sensation rather disturbing, but now she coveted that concentration, wanting it for herself with a selfish yearning. *Wanting* Campion. Ever it came back to that, Joy realized, as her gaze drifted over his powerful form once more, dropping to the hands that rested upon his knees.

Joy wondered what they would feel like upon her, not in the companionable manner of her skating lesson, but as a man touches a woman. She no longer held any illusions about romance, but she had to admit to a curiosity about such things, recently fired by Campion. Her limited experience left her at a loss, and so she imagined touching him instead, sifting her fingers through his hair and exploring beneath his tunic to the hard body below.

Joy shifted, restless in her seat as she took the fantasy farther, envisioning herself in the earl's bed, sharing untold mysteries in the darkness of the night. How would it feel to have those strong arms around her without the fear that he would steal anything of hers, including her independence? Here was an honorable man, a man of the world who might teach her a thing or two.

As Joy sat there, lost in pleasant illusions, an idea evolved slowly, insinuating itself into her mind until she gasped with the audacity of it. And then she wanted to laugh in delight as excitement and relief surged through her, along with a low curl of warmth. Could she?

Why not?

Turning her head slightly, Joy studied the Earl of Campion with a new intensity. By all accounts, he was a man of honor who held himself apart from the common dalliances of others of his gender. She had heard no gossip about him, no rumors of lemans or mistresses, and the knowledge was both pleasing and daunting, for what made her think she could entice him?

Her own formidable will, Joy decided with a smile. Roesia often complained about it, but Joy was driven, and when she wanted something, she usually achieved her goal. She had poured herself into Mallin Fell, turning the small demesne into a stable, if not highly prosperous, holding. And she had managed to keep it, against all odds.

And through the years, Joy had asked for little enough. Faring better than most females, she never complained. She was accustomed to work and always thought of her people first. But now she craved something for herself, and the more she thought about it, the more determined she was to have it, despite the slight twitching of her conscience.

There had been few pleasures in her life; how wrong could it be to want to wring something from this holiday? To know a man's touch for the first time in her life? To finally discover the great mystery? Joy had been glad enough on her wedding night when her boy husband had turned away from her, no more eager than she to consummate their marriage. And she had known no regrets when he had died before growing more into his manhood, leaving her untouched.

A virgin widow.

But now her status seemed ludicrous, and the more Joy considered it, the more she became determined to remedy the situation. She was a curious woman, after all, a seeker of knowledge, so why shouldn't she want to learn from the wisest man she had ever met? With seven sons, the earl ought to know what he was about in the bedchamber, Joy realized, flushing at the thought.

She lifted her chin as she became resolved. Just this once she would take from a man. They owned the world, had harried her most of her life, and owed her more than she could ever claim. It was time she got something worthwhile from their gender and past time she discovered what she had denied herself, Joy thought, with new determination. This Christmas she would give herself a gift.

The Earl of Campion.

CHAPTER FOUR

After the feasting, Joy escaped to the solar, ostensibly to bundle Christmas greenery. In reality, she needed to think. Now that she had made her decision, she only had to execute it, but she had no idea how to lure a man into her bed. With someone like Stephen, she would not need a plan, just a breath in her body, she thought with a grimace. But Campion was no randy rogue. He was a mature man seemingly unaffected by her presence.

Joy frowned, considering all that she had seen of courting behaviors, but those were usually among the lower orders, and she could not imagine plopping herself on the earl's lap with a giggle. Indeed, the idea was so horrifying that she dropped the sprig of holly she had been tying and bent to pick it up. Roesia and Stephen had brought in plenty of bay and holly when they returned from skating, and she and Joy gathered it into bunches of twelve to decorate the hall.

Idly, Joy wondered if Roesia's trip to the pond had been as interesting as her own, and the thought made her pause. Laying the sprig in her lap, Joy slanted a speculative glance toward her attendant. Although younger than herself, Roesia had more experience dealing with men, claiming an appreciation of them that Joy had always disdained, yet now that knowledge might come to good use.

"Roesia, how do you go about making a man... notice you?" Joy asked. The question, although put forward casually enough, caused her attendant to drop her evergreens, scattering small boughs upon the tiled floor.

Eyeing her with a puzzled expression, Roesia knelt to retrieve her work. "Excuse me, my lady, but I thought you asked something about gaining a man's attention!" She laughed, as if amused at her own folly, but the sound died away when she looked at Joy's face.

"You are serious? I was not mistaken?" she asked.

Joy lifted her chin. "I have always sought to increase my store of knowledge by learning from others, but if you are unwilling to share your—"

"Oh, my lady!" Roesia interrupted. "Oh, this is wonderful! But I thought you were resolved against marriage!"

Joy frowned. "I am resolved against it."

"But, you said—"

"I said I was interested in the arts of seduction, not imprisonment," Joy said with a sound of disgust.

Roesia blinked at her in bewilderment. "Surely, you aren't talking about becoming a man's... mistress! You, with all your high ideals about women and all!"

"No, I most certainly will not become a mistress. I won't be around long enough to qualify as that," Joy said, shifting in her seat uncomfortably at the reminder of her more vocal views. "I am thinking of a simple dalliance, the kind that happens all the time at court and even among my neighbors."

Roesia gaped at her openmouthed, and Joy bristled. "You are always prattling on about the pleasures to be found in a man's arms. Now would you deny your words?"

Roesia shook her head. "No, my lady, but I enjoy a good kiss or two now and then and maybe even a tumble with the right fellow, while you've never even looked at a man!"

"Well, now I am," Joy said, her expression righteous.

"And that's all to the good, my lady! But a woman like you wasn't made for a quick toss. Why, I thought you couldn't stand Stephen..." Her words trailed off as she studied Joy. "Oh, my, it's Campion! 'Tis the earl himself who has caught your eye!" Roesia said, lifting a hand to her throat as if she found the discovery shocking.

"And what, pray tell, is wrong with Campion?" Joy said in a dangerously low tone that warned her attendant to watch her speech.

"Nothing, my lady. Truly, nothing. What a man!" Roesia said, with a sigh of appreciation. She seemed lost in thoughts of the earl for so long that Joy scowled at her. And Roesia gave her an apologetic smile before sobering. "But the earl's totally different! You can't take a man like that to your bed and wake up unchanged."

"Whatever do you mean?" Joy asked, genuinely puzzled. Of course, she wanted the experience to change her. She wanted, at last, to be a woman in every sense of the word.

Roesia flushed. "You're talking about simple lust, my lady, but it's not always easy to separate your heart from the rest of you." At Joy's questioning look, she threw up her hands. "What of love, my lady? Not all your fine ideas or stubborn will can protect you against it."

"Love!" Joy scoffed. She had always considered romance a bunch of foolishness conjured by wandering minstrels in order to trade upon the good graces of the lady of the castle. "I fear it not!" she said, with a laugh.

Roesia shook her head. "And what of Campion? He's not like Stephen, eager to get under any woman's skirt! I know more of men than you, my lady, and I tell you that he's not the sort to take a woman to his bed unless he loves her. Do you think he'll just perform like a stallion and then let you go?"

Joy stiffened at the implied threat to her independence. "He will have no choice," she said. "For I am my own woman. He can make no claim upon me."

Roesia sighed as if put upon by a poor student. "My lady, you don't know a thing about males, if you think that. For all that he looks all gentle eyed and calm, the earl has a fierceness in him. Else how could he have ruled these lands and built this dynasty of his? And you ought not give yourself to him unless you mean it. Forever."

Just as Joy opened her mouth to argue, Roesia gave her a hopeful smile. "If you've got your sights set on the earl, why not wed him? That would solve all our problems! And I can't say I'd mind living here," she added with an admiring glance toward the castle's luxurious furnishings.

"I will not marry again," Joy said. She had hated being torn from her home to wed a stranger, had resented her lanky boy of a husband and after his death had come to prize her freedom. Men controlled everything about a wife—her money, her property, her very life. Even friendships between women were discouraged, for a wife must keep her mind upon her duties.

Since the Church decreed that God had made womankind subject to male control, a woman who acted for herself was believed to be possessed by the Devil. And the courts were no more favorable than the Church. If a wife killed her husband, she was executed for treason because her husband was her master, while a man could buy a pardon should he be moved to such violence against his spouse. While men ruled, they conspired to keep women as less than chattel, and no doubt would do so until the end of time, Joy thought bitterly.

"But Campion is no boy forced upon you by relatives," Roesia said. "He's a man, with power aplenty to control his fate, and marrying him would be wholly different. No more worries over the harvest or holding your demesne or *anything.*" Roesia sighed at the notion, and Joy felt a bitter guilt at the lean years. She had done her best to run the small household and bit of lands surrounding it without help from anyone, but she had precious few funds and there was always something to eat away at them.

Oblivious to her thoughts, Roesia smiled wickedly. "And since you've a taste for the earl, you could ease it every night, or day for that matter!"

Joy frowned at her attendant's exuberance. "As appealing as that notion is," she answered dryly, "I am hardly ready to give up my life for it."

"But the earl's not like most men! He thinks differently, having read so many books and all. And you don't see him treating anyone badly."

It was true. Campion seemed wise and understanding, but as her husband, he would still own her, and Joy refused to submit to anyone's possession. She had struggled to make a life for herself at her small manor, a life in which she had all that she needed.

As if reading her thoughts, Roesia glanced about the well-appointed solar, a far cry from the close quarters to which they were accustomed. "And this castle is the most beautiful place I've ever seen, with so many lovely things. Why, living here would be like living a dream," her attendant said.

"For you, perhaps. But for me it would be bondage, of a sort, and I am not bargaining away my freedom for furnishings in my hall and delicacies upon my table."

Roesia sighed as she reached for a ribbon to tie around her bundle of greenery. "You're a hard woman, my lady. I just hope that you won't one day rue those precious views of yours, for they won't keep you warm on a cold night."

Her words turned Joy's thoughts toward Campion, and she imagined his strong body heating hers, holding the chill and all else at bay. It was a tantalizing notion, but one which she dismissed with a frown. An extra fur would work as well, she told herself firmly. And it would be a lot less trouble in the bargain.

Irritated with her attendant, Joy returned to the hall, where she spent the evening weaving the rest of the greenery around a wooden frame into a kissing bush. Roesia had been no help at all. In fact, the woman who had perpetually urged her to find a man now refused to aid Joy in gaining his attention. Capricious creature!

Although Campion had reigned over the light supper served earlier, he had disappeared since, and Joy knew a sense of disappointment, along with annoyance at herself. When had she ever cared about a man's movements, as long as they did not jeopardize her home? Perhaps since she had decided to learn how to lure one to her bed, she thought wryly.

But without the man's presence, she could only sit back and stew, a disturbing sensation that made her wonder just how much she was investing in this little plan of hers. It was near sunset, and the holiday revelry was winding to a close as the villeins and freemen who had spent the day at the castle prepared to take their leave.

Stephen was acting the gregarious host, and Joy debated

whether to ask him or his brother where their father had gone. While part of her rebelled at seeking out any man, another part declared such knowledge necessary to the fulfillment of her plan. Wracked by unaccustomed confusion, Joy finished the bush with an impatient gesture.

She looked up, prepared to call a servant over to hang it, only to find Stephen standing in front of her. Too close. There was nowhere to go, and the massive chair was too heavy to slide backward. Besides, it was not in her nature to give ground to a man, so she simply lifted her chin and gave him a quelling look. To her annoyance, he placed his hands on the table on either side of her, effectively hedging her in as he loomed over her.

"Beautiful, work, my lady. Shall we try it?" he asked, in a low voice, tilting his dark head toward the bush. And before Joy could answer, he lowered his mouth to hers.

The mistletoe lodged among the evergreen boughs, ribbons, and nuts was supposed to promote the kiss of peace, but this was no friendly brush of the lips. Stephen's was a kiss of seduction, his lips moving expertly over her own, and Joy, a stranger to such things, gasped in surprise.

To her astonishment, Stephen seized the opportunity to thrust his tongue into her mouth. He tasted of wine and bitterness, the cold calculation of his movements fueling her outrage, and Joy pulled back at the same time that she lifted her knee.

Although she had little experience in kissing, she knew how to protect herself, and she heard Stephen's yelp of pain as she slipped from his embrace. Watching him warily, she saw him teeter precariously before plunging toward the table. Only the innate de Burgh grace saved him from smashing his handsome face into the worn wood, and Joy spared him no sympathy.

Reynold grunted in amusement, and Stephen turned his head, his handsome face surly, but Joy lifted her chin, meeting his glare with her own until he shoved away from the table. His easy smile returning, he bowed his head toward her. "Touché, lady," he said softly, before turning to go.

"Coddled whelp," Joy murmured, but she held her ground until he disappeared up the stairs, then she sank back down into her chair with a sigh at the vagaries of fate. She did not want the son's interest, but the father's! It was only after her gaze fell upon the abandoned kissing bush that a slow smile crept over her face.

Stephen had given her what Roesia would not—a lesson in seduction— and Joy seized upon the tempting idea, hoping that her efforts worked better than Stephen's. As the plan took root she ignored her own trepidation and rose to her feet, walking toward the servant who was removing the last cups of ale from the trestle tables.

"Wilda?" Joy asked. At the woman's wary nod, she smiled. "I wondered if you knew where Lord Campion might be."

"Taking a bath, I gather, though why the men of this family feel such a need to be clean I will never know. Why, it's not natural!" the servant confided, before realizing that she might have said too much. She glanced away, her eyes downcast as she reached for another up. "Probably something he read in those foreign books of his," she muttered.

"Or a man's sport," Joy said dryly. She knew that oftentimes male bathers had women attendants, which could lead to more than washing.

Wilda immediately shook her head at the implication. "Oh, you won't find anything of that here, my lady!" she declared. "His lordship and all the boys are good men. Oh, Stephen's a bit of a rogue, but how can he help it when all the females adore him?"

Joy could have argued with that, but she was relieved to learn that the earl was as honorable as she had judged him.

"Lord Campion ought to be back down soon, for he likes to keep an eye on his hall, to make sure the celebrating doesn't go on all night," Wilda said with a grin.

"Thank you. I think I will wait to... speak with him."

"Yes, my lady," Wilda said, resuming her work.

Turning, Joy walked slowly back to the high table, where

she idly fingered the kissing bush. Around her the festivities were coming to an end, servants cleaning away debris and dousing candles so that soon the massive vaulted space was in shadow. Taking a seat in Campion's chair, Joy watched Reynold usher out a few straggling knights before he sought his own rest. Then some of the servants began making up pallets on the other side of the room, so far away that they disappeared into darkness.

Night was coming at last to Campion Castle. Where was the earl? Joy knew an odd sensation that she ascribed to anticipation, not to overwrought nerves. But when, at last, she heard footsteps, she flinched, regretting her impulsive decision. Turning, she saw Campion standing on the stairs, surveying his domain, and the very sight of him flooded her with warmth. Any doubts she had entertained fled swiftly as she rose to her feet.

"Campion." It felt wonderful to speak his name, but Joy knew a possessive need to discover his first name, his true name, and whisper it to him in the privacy of his chamber. She shivered.

"Lady Warwick. I am surprised to find you here so late," the earl said. Concern colored his voice, and Joy wanted to be rid of it—and all else that stood between them.

"How do you like it?" she asked, moving aside to reveal her work. Campion looked at her, and for a moment, she saw a glimpse of vulnerability behind those all-knowing eyes, a look of slumbering... something. But then it was gone, replaced by his maddeningly courteous demeanor.

Courtesy be hanged, Joy thought, with mutinous glance. She wanted to scream and shout and drag a reaction from Campion that was more than polite welcome, that was even a small measure of the heat she felt in his presence. Instead, she gestured toward the table. "Here. Come see your Christmas bush," she said. "What think you of it?"

Campion stepped forward, his innate grace making his movements fluid as his tall form was cast in shadow, and Joy swallowed. As he studied her creation, she inched closer.

When he turned his head to find her next to him, he cleared his throat, staring down at her with a certain intensity that gave her hope. "Lovely," he said.

"Do you think so?" Joy asked, her breath quickening at his nearness. Even in the dim glow of the remaining candles, she could see his broad shoulders, the elegant way in which he held himself. She wanted to reach out and touch him.

"Then we must make use of it," she murmured. A surge of power ran through her that she would never have associated with the role of seductress, and she liked it well.

Campion lifted his brows in polite query. Too polite.

"A kiss," Joy said.

Surprise glinted his eyes. "Certainly." But to Joy's chagrin, he did not look one bit excited by the prospect. He was at his most dignified, the earl, and he bent his head as if to brush her cheek, but a glancing touch of peace was not what Joy wanted. She was blossoming in her new role, and at the last moment, she turned to meet his lips with her own.

They were warm and firm and so very delicious that Joy grabbed onto his tunic to pull herself closer. She tried to remember just how Stephen had managed to get inside her mouth, but it was awfully hard to keep her mind on her task when she felt so odd, all fiery and alive.

Campion went still and for a moment, Joy thought he would push her away, just as she had done to his son. She made a low sound of protest, but then his mouth opened over hers, his arms came around her, and his breath mingled with hers in exquisite union.

Joy moved against him, her arms circling his broad chest as his tongue meshed with hers, for Campion took the kiss beyond Stephen's calculated efforts. No cool display of expertise was this, but a passion that rivaled her own. One of his hands moved behind her head, as if to hold her in place, while the other stroked her back, lower and lower still, until it closed around her buttocks and lifted her. Joy felt the hot, hard length of him rub her stomach, and she wiggled against it, wanting more. It was shocking and primitive and so exciting that she cried out in glorious surrender.

And then it was over. Just as suddenly as it had been unleashed, Campion's potent ardor was restrained once more. Joy, whimpering a protest, realized that he was setting her away, gently but firmly. She had but a glimpse of his stricken expression before he turned his head away.

"Forgive me. I had no right, no call to..." He broke off, and when he swiveled toward her, she saw that he had assumed his usual dignity. "You must seek your chamber. It is late, and you are without your attendant."

That was my intention! Joy wanted to scream. "But—"

"There is no excuse for my behavior."

"But—"

Someone moved at the entrance to the kitchens, and the earl, with seemingly preternatural recognition, called softly. "Wilda, would you please escort Lady Warwick to her chamber?"

"Yes, my lord," came the reply, and Joy wanted to shriek in frustration. So much for her seduction attempt! But what could she do? Tell Wilda to mind her own business? Press the earl back upon the high table and force him to appease her desires? The very notion horrified her, and lifting her chin, Joy went, chagrined at her rejection.

But even as she stalked away, she knew that for one precious moment she had felt the earth move, and she had moved Campion, too, whether he willed it or not.

Campion arose early after a uneasy night filled with images of his guest which, while enthralling, left him feeling angry with himself. Even in the light of dawn, the memory of their embrace plagued him, and he groaned. What had possessed him? He could not recall ever acting so impulsively, so *wildly.* It was simply not his nature. Perhaps he was growing old and mad.

He stayed in his chamber, unwilling to face the revelries, at least until the feasting began again, but paced the length of the room with a restlessness he had not known in years. It was in this state that Reynold found him, and his son's innocent inquiry after his health annoyed him beyond endurance.

"I am fine," Campion muttered. *I am a fully functioning man, who realizes what he has been missing and now must fight the craving for what he cannot have.* He stood at the window, hands clasped behind his back, and stared out at the bleak landscape below, enjoying the chill wind upon his face. *Mayhap it would cool his hot blood.*

Behind him he heard Reynold take a seat on the settle near the hearth. "'Tis looking more like Christmas in the hall," his son said. "Already the knights have made use of the kissing bush."

At Reynold's mention of the greenery that held the mistletoe, Campion felt a flush scald his cheekbones. The memory of Lady Warwick in his arms, his hand buried in her thick hair, made him clear his throat.

"That is as it should be, as long as the celebrations do not get out of hand," Campion said. He was a fine one to talk, he thought, for as lord it was up to him to set an example for his subjects. Last night he had set a poor one, should anyone have seen him with Lady Warwick in the shadows, and the knowledge that his actions may have injured his visitor's reputation made them doubly regretful.

"Stephen tried it out first," Reynold said in a deceptively careless tone that made Campion turn to look at him. "With the lady herself."

Campion stiffened. "Lady Warwick?"

Reynold nodded. "You know Stephen, always one for the women, whether they want him or not."

Campion held his tongue for a long moment as he tried to divine Reynold's meaning. "Are you saying that Stephen *forced* himself upon our guest?" His fury mixed with his own guilt, for had he not done the same?

"Well, he didn't hurt her. In fact, she hurt him. First, she drove a knee into his groin, and then she practically knocked him face-first into the high table. It was highly entertaining, though I suspect his pride was injured more than anything else."

Campion was glad he had not been present, for it had been a long time since he had brawled with one of his sons, and right now he had an overpowering urge to thrash Stephen. "Where is he?"

Reynold shrugged. "Off with someone who is not as immune to his charms."

"When he reappears, I will have him apologize," Campion said to himself. Then he eyed his son carefully, wondering at Reynold's motives. The boys always held together, keeping each other's mischief from their sire. What had compelled Reynold to speak? "Thank you for telling me," Campion said.

Reynold shrugged and rose to his feet. "Lady Warwick seems able to take care of herself, but I thought you should know that she came away from the encounter looking as if she had just tasted rancid meat." Reynold grunted in amusement and turned to go, leaving Campion staring after him.

Had Lady Warwick looked the same after she left him last night? No, he could still hear her low cry of pleasure, feel her pressing against him... Or was that what he wished to recall? With a frown, Campion knew he owed his guest an apology, not just for his son, but for himself. What must she think of the de Burghs? he wondered, with a shudder.

Campion found her in the solar with her attendant, sewing small figures, presumably for the kissing bush, and he rued their bargain, especially considering what had come of her handiwork. Standing in the doorway unobserved, he took a moment to admire the guest who had wrought so much havoc among his household.

Although young and beautiful, Joy looked far too somber to arouse such passions, making Campion wish that he could remove the line that blotted her brow and the tension in her mouth. What mysteries lay behind her serious demeanor? He would ease her cares, if only she would confide in him, but she kept her own counsel and with such fierce independence that he would not presume to intrude.

Then, as if his perusal alerted her to his presence, she glanced up to see him, and Campion was rewarded with a smile that struck him so forcefully, he hardly noticed her nod of dismissal to her attendant. “No, Lady, you need not send Roesia away,” he protested, as the woman passed him, leaving him alone with Lady Warwick in the cozy room.

Unnerved, Campion drew upon his dignity and approached his guest, bowing his head in greeting. “Lady, I have just had some grievous news,” he said. At her startled expression, he moved forward to halt in front of her.

“Nay, nothing tragic, but nonetheless, disturbing,” he said. “I have learned that Stephen treated you ill last night, followed by my own inexcusable actions. I apologize, and Stephen will, too. As a guest in my home, you should be inviolate, safe and secure from any sort of imposition, and I assure you nothing of the kind will happen again during your stay.”

Instead of thanking him tearfully, Joy shrugged off his words as though they were of little import. “I will be pleased to hear Stephen’s repentance, but I require no apology from you for a boon I begged myself. And might beg again?” she asked, lifting her hand to reveal a small sprig of mistletoe, which she dangled above them.

Campion had not made a name for himself by being caught off guard, but he was hard pressed not to gape in astonishment. Surely, this lovely young woman did not mean she wanted him to kiss her? Why would she reject Stephen in one breath and tease him in the next? She waited, expectantly, while Campion struggled for a polite reply.

“My dear lady, I am most...” *What?* Flattered? Surprised? For once, the earl was at a loss for words. “Tempted. However, after last night, I think you will agree that it would be wiser to refrain from these holiday rituals with Stephen or myself.”

“I am not interested in Stephen,” she said. She spoke in that direct way of hers, her violet gaze challenging, and if Campion didn't know better he would think she was proclaiming her interest in... himself. "Lady," he said, chiding her gently. "You cannot know what you are about. You are a young and vibrant and beautiful woman, while I have sons older than those you have met, seven sons in all, and grandchildren!"

"Ah, so that means you no longer are attracted to women?" she asked, her lips tilting in an echo of his own chiding expression.

Campion frowned. "Of course not. I find you most attractive." Intriguing. *Arousing.* "But surely you would prefer someone nearer your own age, like Reynold or Stephen." Campion nearly choked on their names, unwilling to urge the lady toward either, but he was determined to be sensible.

At the mention of his sons, she dropped all pretense of teasing, granting him that direct gaze he so admired. "Stephen and Reynold are both still boys, despite their ages, and we both know it," she said, before turning to move gracefully toward the hearth.

Stunned, Campion felt he ought to defend his sons, but he suspected she was all too right in her assessment. Although full-grown knights, they lacked the maturity of some of their brothers.

Silently, Campion watched her circle the room, each step charming and assured, until she paused before the window. "I've had a boy, and I find I would prefer a man," she said, turning her head toward him, and Campion's mouth went dry.

Never before had he been treated to such bold speech. Oh, there had been ladies at court, with their subtle and not so subtle pursuits, but most of their intrigues had left him cold. Lady Warwick spoke with a forthrightness that left no doubt as to her intent, yet somehow her words were not brazen, nor were her actions. Campion sensed that she was not the sort to make a habit of dalliances. She spoke of a boy. Had he been her husband? And now... Campion?

His body responded to that idea, and he took a deep breath in an effort to control it. As the man, older and more experienced, it was up to him to put a stop to this nonsense. Despite her air of composure, she was too young and unworldly to know what she was doing, whether she intended a kiss or... something more.

"Lady—"

"Joy. Please call me Joy."

"Joy." Her name slid far too easily off of his tongue, for Campion thought of her as bringing joy to his holiday, along with other more complex emotions. Although she seemed at once too serious and too willful for her name, it suited her. *Joy.*

"And you are?"

Campion stilled, stunned for a moment by her request. When he spoke, he did so automatically, without pausing to consider the wisdom of granting her such an intimacy. "Fawke."

"Fawke." She spoke in a low voice that skittered along his nerve endings to rouse both his lower body and the heart he had thought better schooled after all these years. How long had it been since someone had called him that?

Staring at the slight figure who stood gazing out his solar window, Campion had the sudden, eerie sensation that he was meeting his fate, and all that he might do would simply delay the inevitable. He shook the feeling aside and cleared his throat, striving to regain his reason.

"Joy, you can hardly be serious about this..." *Flirtation? Kiss? Bedding?* Again, Campion was at a loss for words.

"And why not?" she asked over her shoulder. Campion watched the gentle sway of her black curls and felt his body tighten treasonously. "I was wed at age fifteen, an arrangement to keep property in the family. He was twelve." Her tone was flat, but Campion sensed her resentment and added his own. Although such alliances were not uncommon, he did not approve of marriages involving children of either gender.

"Not a year later, he was gored by a wild boar, and I've been a widow ever since. During all that time I have never had any desire to remarry, nor any desire to share myself with a man." As the startling revelation of her words struck him,

Campion found that she had turned to face him once more, her chin lifted in that familiar expression of defiance. "So don't tell me what I want or don't want. I'm a grown woman. I know my own mind."

What Joy would have done or said next, Campion didn't know, for at that point his steward entered, anxiously wishing to consult with her about some petty detail of the feast. Something about candles? Effortlessly sliding into the role of chatelaine that had been assigned her, she moved toward the man, her soft replies barely discernible to Campion, whose mind was still focused on something else entirely. As if aware of his thoughts, Joy gave him a nod and a smile before following his steward from the room with a grace, confidence, and allure unequaled.

Campion stood there staring after her, feeling as if his mouth were hanging open from their encounter. Joy wanted *him?* Joy *wanted* him. He drew a deep breath, tamping down the elation that swept through him and replacing it with a more appropriate response.

He had not held his earldom by succumbing to impulse or irrational behavior, no matter how tempting. Unlike his son Stephen, Campion did not engage in brief liaisons, and despite the admiration and attraction he felt for his Christmas guest, he had nothing else to offer her.

The truth was that he had no intention of taking another wife, and, even if he did, Joy was too young. Too beautiful. Too alive. Too stubborn. Too *everything.*

CHAPTER FIVE

After what happened in the solar, Campion kept a careful, if cordial distance from his guest during her stay. But he still delighted in her company. He had decided that she was too somber and was determined that she learn to enjoy herself while visiting his demesne. The day before, he had encouraged her to join in the games that were part of the Christmas celebration, and tonight, having learned that she did not play chess, he was taking great pleasure in teaching her.

Joy was an adept pupil. Already, during their second game, she was evincing a remarkable talent for the strategy necessary to win. She was a fascinating creature, Campion mused as they sat before the hearth, the chess table between them. Concentrating on her next move, her dainty fingers hovering over the pieces, she was more beautiful than anyone he had ever seen.

Campion knew that "fair" was used to describe women with blond tresses, but none of those ladies could rival Joy with her dark locks hanging loose and heavy. His son Dunstan's wife had brown curls, but Joy's were black as night, the sleek long locks seeming to possess a life of their own as they fell clear to her waist.

For all the delicacy of her features, she was a strong-willed, capable woman. And despite her bold speech, there was an air of innocence about her, as if she had missed out on so much of life, including the activities she deemed frivolous. Had she suffered a hard existence? Her clothes were fine enough and her train well-manned. Joy was a puzzle, and one he would enjoy unraveling, if he had the time.

And therein lay the cause of Campion's unease, for this evening marked the fifth day of Christmas, with only seven remaining. Although Joy seemed to enjoy their play well enough, what would happen when she left? Would she return to a life of toil? Campion found his thoughts more and more occupied with her departure and the future that would follow.

It was only natural that he be concerned with the welfare of one of his guests, but Joy was not the sort of woman who would answer questions about her situation. She was intensely private, another trait which he admired, yet he found himself wanting to penetrate that privacy, to establish an intimacy with her that no one else could claim. In a paternal sort of way, Campion told himself, even as his gaze followed the brush of her slender fingers against her bishop.

"Very good!" he said, when he saw her placement of the piece. "You are an excellent student."

Her answering smile nearly stole his breath, and Campion swiftly moved his own piece and tilted back, putting some distance between them. But Joy only leaned closer, her voice so low that he had to bend near to hear her.

"It occurs to me that if you are so determined that I learn all these games of which you are so fond, perhaps there is another manner of play you can teach me, that would be even more pleasurable for us both," she said, her violet eyes like pools under those thick lashes. Her husky whisper caused an immediate reaction in Campion's body, but he cleared his throat, ignoring the provocative suggestion.

"Watch your queen," he advised, without daring to look at her. Despite his best efforts, he was plagued by desire when Joy was present and inappropriate thoughts when she was not. Her teasing comments did not help, and he was finding it more and more difficult to keep a tight rein on himself.

Campion shifted in his seat. He had loved both of his wives. He had been very young when he wed the first time and more mature when he married Anne, and yet he could not recall feeling this... unsettled by either one. Both had been gentle souls, but Joy was different. Her look of cool composure hid a fiery spirit with a core of steel. She would make a fit wife for any man, Campion thought, before catching himself.

Perhaps he had been without a woman too long, for there had been no one since his last visit to court. Yet he had not felt the lack. He did not believe in allowing passions to rule one's life, so long ago had suppressed such yearnings. But now, it was as if his dormant desires wished to make up for long periods of celibacy as soon as possible. *With Joy.* It was aggravating... and vaguely exhilarating.

"Check," she said, warning of her intent to capture, and Campion looked up in surprise to see her sly smile. She was referring to the chess board, of course. Then why did he have the impression she meant something else entirely?

Stephen glanced at the cozy scene by the hearth and frowned at his brother "She has him rattled," he muttered.

"Who? Father?" Reynold let out a rough sound that was the closest he came to laughter. "Campion is never rattled."

"Yes, he is," Stephen said. Reynold was too young to recall his mother's death and Campion's long vigil in her chamber, but Stephen remembered it as a chilling time when even his all-wise father seemed to be lost.

He shrugged off the memory and took a drink. "I've seen it before, but I never thought to see it again. He hasn't been shaken from his usual stoicism for years. Until now. Until *her*."

Reynold snorted. "You're just piqued that the lady won't notice you."

"Well, I have to admit that there's something wrong when a beautiful young woman pays more attention to my father than me," Stephen said, with a nod toward the duo by the fire. "I wonder what she's up to."

"Nothing," Reynold scoffed. "Do you think that any woman who is interested in Father must have an ulterior motive? You're daft!"

"He's a powerful man," Stephen said. "While I'm nothing but a younger son with no prospects."

Reynold snorted. "If you would get your head out of your wine cup long enough—"

"Don't start on me, when you should look to yourself!"

Reynold grunted, but did not rise to the bait. "Father is still a handsome fellow to the ladies. Haven't you heard Marion coo about him enough to know that? Just because he's lived like a monk these last years doesn't mean he is one."

"A scary thought," Stephen said. "Surely you aren't suggesting that the almighty Campion might have needs like the rest of us mere mortals?"

Reynold muttered a low oath. "Can't you see *anything* around you except yourself?" His gaze swung toward the hearth and back to Stephen. "He's lonely, and she's good for him. Leave them be."

With a black look, Reynold left the table, much to the disappointment of his brother. Stephen never would admit as much, but he found himself missing Simon, who could always be counted upon for a good quarrel. But Simon was off with his wife, and Reynold, who did not suffer an excess of bile, just wasn't as much fun.

And as for Reynold's insinuation that Campion felt the same as less exalted beings, Stephen doubted it. He glanced toward the fire and shook his head before lifting his cup to drink. Still, she had the earl rattled, he had no doubt of that.

It was the sixth day of Christmas, and Joy's frustration was mounting. Although she sensed that Campion was not indifferent to her, he maintained a strict decorum that left her no opportunity to test his remarkable restraint. She had hoped for another cozy game of chess, but tonight he had talked her into playing Hoodman's Bluff, and so she was standing in the midst of the hall, blindfolded, while the other players turned her around several times.

Laughing at a momentary dizziness, Joy felt her tension ease. Although she could not imagine engaging in such nonsense at home, here at Campion everything, even the most foolish of pastimes, took on a magical glow, whether from the season or the castle. Or Campion. At the thought of the stubborn earl, Joy smiled. The object of this game was to find and identify someone without the aid of sight, and she knew just whom she would seek.

Ignoring the loud encouragement of those close by, Joy

moved away from the crowd, for she knew Campion would be on the periphery, watching quietly with those enigmatic eyes. He would not be jostling others or frantically hopping about for attention. He would be still, his power leashed with dignity.

"You're heading for the kitchens, lady!" someone called, and indeed, Joy recognized the odor of food drifting toward her. Her outstretched fingers brushed against a man's chest, but the softness of it made her turn away. There was no softness about the earl, except inside him, where goodness and honor and gentleness dwelt. Moving on to much laughter and teasing, Joy found the wooden screen that stood at the end of the hall near the entrance to the buttery and the kitchens.

There she stopped, as a faint whiff of something else caught her attention. Suddenly, the game and its noisy participants all faded away. In the darkness she felt alone with the man she had sought, whose scent she recognized as well as her own. She could sense his presence, his strength, and the smell of him: clean clothing, the spicy soap that he used, and that which was his alone. She had known it before in the darkness of the hall by the kissing bush, and now she reached unerringly out to it again.

Joy was aware of the sound of the crowd, but only as an irritating rumble, for she was focused solely on the earl. With one more step she felt his heat, her hands lifting to rest upon his broad chest. As she stood there, Joy wished that she could remain where she was always, that he would take her in his arms and hold her. *Keep her.*

Someone pulled off the hood, but Joy stayed in front of Campion, and amid shrieks and cheers, the game continued, moving away from the dim area at the end of the hall. Drawing him with her, Joy backed behind the carved screen that would hide them from prying eyes.

There, in the sheltered shadows, Joy tried her hand at a new game, one far more dear to her, as her fingers slid up Campion's chest into the sleek softness of his dark hair. She stroked it with wonder, despite his stillness and the intense regard of his brown eyes.

Along with the usual warmth that came with his nearness, Joy felt something more, a sweetness that seemed to fill her, pressing behind her eyes until she wanted to weep with the pleasure of touching him. Roesia's warning came back to her, but she wondered if it were not too late to heed her attendant, for she already had come to care for this man.

Recklessly, Joy raised herself up on her toes and touched her mouth to his, and it was even more wonderful than she remembered. The kiss was an exploration, a greeting well met that nonetheless sent heat surging through her, and her arms slipped around his waist, anchoring her to his strength.

After a moment's hesitation, Campion kissed the corner of her mouth, her eyelashes, her brows, and the line of her jaw, murmuring her name in a tone that she never heard before. It was a whisper that spoke of awe and desire, and Joy responded with abandon, pressing her body against his and welcoming his lips with her own. She recognized now the hard ridge of his manhood against her stomach, and she wanted nothing more than to feel all of him, around her, inside her, as part of her.

"Let us go to your chamber," she urged breathlessly against his cheek, but he stiffened even as she spoke. Joy could sense the withdrawal of his passion, and she whimpered in protest. Still he set her away. Even in the shadows, she could see the glint of his eyes, shining with wisdom and passion withheld.

"It would not be right," he said.

"But I want you. I… I care for you," Joy said. At her faltering confession, his expression softened, and he reached out to stroke her hair in a gesture of comfort that only made her desire more.

"Nay. 'Tis but a passing thing, and I would be a rogue if I were to take advantage of it," he said.

His words made Joy bristle, and she shrugged off his hand. "Do not speak to me as if I were a child, for I am not! I am a woman full grown, a widow who has maintained a holding for years! Why do you not credit my decision? Do you think I'm a fool?"

"No, of course not," he said, in gentle placation that only made Joy angrier.

"Then why do you dispute me? Why can't I know my own mind? If I chose Reynold, would you fault me?" Joy saw the flicker of emotion that crossed his face, and was well glad of it. She wanted to hurt him, to punish him for denying her.

"No," he said softly, then he turned away, releasing a heavy sigh into the shadows. "The problem, as you've divined, bright lady that you are, is with me. I married twice and loved and lost both of my wives. And after I buried Anne, I vowed never to put myself in such a position again."

Stunned by his admission, Joy came up behind him, placing a palm against his broad back. She had glimpsed a vulnerability in this strong man, but she had never imagined that he had forsaken women to avoid the pain of another's death. How could she argue against such sentiment? She slid her arms around his waist and rested her cheek against him.

"Foolish man, you are always complaining about my age," she muttered into his tunic. "Now see how it can only be to your advantage, for I will surely outlive you anyway!"

Campion stiffened, then turned toward her, and Joy was afraid her audacious response had been too much. But he only shook his head and started laughing, a deep rumble of merriment that gladdened her heart. It seemed the perfect opportunity for a kiss or more, to lay claim to this man and convince him to join her in bed, but his admission gave her pause.

She might care for him, but Joy was still determined to leave, and although it was hardly the same as dying, would Campion be hurt by her defection? He valued loyalty and honor, as did she, so why did she feel as if her plans to go were both disloyal and dishonorable?

And so when their moment of quiet intimacy was disturbed by servants bringing the wassail from the kitchens, Joy said nothing, caught in a coil of her own making as surely as Roesia had predicted.

Jostled to his senses by the wassailers, Campion held out his hand to Joy, whose sudden, stricken expression made him rue his words. He never should have talked about his grief for Anne. It was an ill-mannered man who spoke to one woman of another, and yet, his wives were a part of him and Joy should know it. Perhaps that knowledge would remind her of the differences between them.

But even as he tried to hold on to the vow he had made, Campion felt his resolve slipping away. Other men his age took young wives, oftentimes to give them heirs, and although he had plenty of those already, Campion knew no one would fault him for marrying a woman of Joy's years. It was more difficult to consider loving again, but already she had slipped beneath his reserve to nudge at his heart—and elsewhere.

As his fingers closed over hers, Campion felt the surge of heat that came simply from touching her. Would that he could lead her upstairs to his chamber! She had offered herself up to him, and his body clamored to accept, but he held firm.

It would not be right. There was too much standing between them, even more yet unknown, and Campion couldn't shake his feeling that she was keeping something from him. Nor could he dismiss his initial impression that Joy was not the best judge of what was best for her, at least in this instance. She did not strike him as impulsive and might well rue her impulsive decision,

So, instead of taking her to his bed, Campion escorted her to the chair beside his own, where the rousing game of Hoodman's Bluff was coming to an end. A glance over the tables below told him that the revelers were growing weary and that Stephen, slumped in one of the chairs, was drunk. It was not surprising these days, especially during the festivities, but Campion saw the reckless gleam in his eye and frowned.

He had reason to be proud of all his sons, Stephen included, but right now his patience with the boy's antics was running low. And, along with the exasperation, he felt a familiar guilt that he had somehow failed his son. Perhaps if there had been more of a woman's presence in the household, he thought, and his eyes traveled, unbidden, to Joy.

She spoke of wanting him, but for how long? Barring more ill weather, in only a few more days she would be gone, and they had not talked about extending her visit. Although he ought to be relieved to see an end to his temptation, all he felt was a gnawing despair, as if the lady represented his last chance for her namesake. Joy.

Campion realized that his own perusal had drawn Stephen's, and he felt a sudden, unreasoning proprietorship. *His Joy,* he thought, even as he recognized the reaction as rather barbaric. Although he had told her often enough to choose someone closer to her own age, now he wanted to deny it, to shout his possession to the world, and only great force of will kept him in his seat.

One of the wassailers stopped by his chair, wishing him prosperity in the coming year, and although Campion turned and smiled, his thoughts remained with those at the high table. He wondered from whence came his passion, for he could not recall ever feeling so deeply, so violently.

"You're going about it the wrong way, you know," Stephen drawled, making Campion wonder what his son was up to now.

"What?" Joy's soft reply followed, and Campion listened intently even as he nodded at the fellow raising his cup in song before him.

"You'll never lure Campion into marriage by pursuing him." Stephen's snide comment made the earl jerk his head toward his son, the wassailer forgotten.

"I have no interest in marrying the earl," Joy said, and the rebuke that Campion was forming for his son died on his lips. *She didn't want to marry him?*

Stephen continued as if Joy had not spoken. "He's too noble to marry a pretty young thing like you. Now, if you were in desperate straits, in need of a husband to protect you, then you can be sure the honorable earl would do the right thing, no matter what his personal feelings."

Both stunned and appalled by his son's words, Campion nonetheless recognized the truth of them. If Joy needed him in some way, he would gladly seize the excuse to make her his, and the knowledge did not sit well upon his shoulders.

"Why not plead your case, Lady Warwick?" Stephen asked, inclining his head toward Campion."Why not be honest and explain that you left your home, rushing into a snowstorm, in order to avoid the arrival of your uncle, who has been pressing you to marry again. Another cousin of his perhaps? Someone you liked no better than your first husband?" he asked, his mobile mouth moving into a hard line.

Campion's gaze swiveled toward Joy. Did Stephen speak the truth of things? Few monied widows were allowed to remain so for long, if they had male relatives or liege lords who would benefit from their remarriage. A widow with no children and a decent holding would be worth a nice settlement though she would see none of it. Although Campion had wondered at Joy's freedom, her strength and assurance had fooled him. He had thought her wholly independent, not a woman under siege.

No wonder she had turned to him.

Campion felt a stir of disappointment. He had thought Joy's desire for him was genuine, if misguided, but now he saw her overtures for what they were: the actions of an intelligent woman trying to save herself from another bad marriage.

He could hardly blame her, nor did she lose his respect, yet he felt a sharp pain, a prick of more than his pride. But it was swiftly overwhelmed by his innate sense of honor. Here was a lady in distress, a lovely, educated, capable woman who sought his protection. And he had denied her.

"Was it just happenstance that led you here, or were you hunting better game?" Stephen drawled. "Perhaps someone who wouldn't care that you might be barren?"

Rage beyond reason surging though him at Stephen's taunt, Campion shot to his feet and laid his hands on the table. "That is enough." It was all he trusted himself to say.

Stephen's gaze swung round, as if he had all but forgotten his sire's presence and was stunned by the rebuke. Their gazes locked for a long moment until, with a low grunt, Stephen picked up his cup and drank. Around them, the silence was deafening, and Campion gestured for the wassailers to begin anew. When they did, he once more took his seat and turned his attention to the woman beside him.

"Is it true?" he asked gently. Joy's head was bent, her face obscured by her luxurious midnight hair, and Campion had the horrible suspicion that she was weeping.

She quickly disabused him of that notion, lifting her chin to reveal a fierce expression. "Perhaps. But what if it is?" she asked, as if in challenge. "'Tis not the first time Hobart has harried me to take a husband, and I'm sure it will not be the last. But do you see me wed? Nay."

She rose to her feet, magnificent in her controlled fury, and whirled toward Stephen. "Since 'tis my business and not yours, Stephen de Burgh, I will keep my own counsel. But let me assure you that I am fully capable of handling my uncle and have done so for years. Dare you imagine otherwise?"

The look she gave Stephen made him squirm in his seat, a feat few could manage, and without waiting for a reply, she turned on her heel and stalked from the room with a dignity that stole Campion's breath.

He had been right all along. Not only had she kept something from him, but she was too much for him. Too beautiful, too willful, too independent, and too passionate—for him to resist.

He knew what he must do.

CHAPTER SIX

Campion awoke on the eve of the new year with a new purpose. He had learned long ago that choosing one's moment was vital, so he had not pursued Joy when she left the hall the night before. She was a stubborn woman, more so when angry, and he gave her time to recover from her outrage in the hope that she would be able to see reason, come the morning.

As for himself, Campion had made his own decision, for in the face of Joy's dilemma, his resolve not to marry again had fallen by the wayside. He told himself he was doing the honorable thing, but it was the threat of another taking his place that spurred him to action. The mere thought of her going to someone else's bed, of marrying a man of her uncle's choosing, was enough to rouse his blood to a fever pitch. She was *his Joy*.

No longer startled by such violent sentiments in connection with his guest, Campion did his best to wrestle them into submission, cloaking his passion in dignity. He had prepared his arguments and, confident of his success, he sought her out.

She was in the solar with her attendant, and the earl took a moment to admire her beauty before he was discovered. Roesia immediately rose to leave, and Joy, eyeing him with something akin to alarm, voiced her protest. But it went unheeded, and soon he was alone with the woman who would be his wife.

The rebellious look she gave him boded ill, and Campion knew a sudden, swift disappointment, for he missed the welcome he once had seen in her expression. Had it been an illusion, as Stephen claimed? Campion only knew he wanted to bring it back, fool that he was. When she pursued him, he had decried it, but now he missed his bold seductress. *His Joy.*

"I apologize once more for any distress that my family has caused you," he said softly, cursing both Stephen and himself. But Joy only shrugged and turned away, a movement that struck Campion painfully, and he moved to sit before her upon a low stool.

"Why did you not confide in me?" he asked, without accusation.

"Do all who tarry here share their most personal problems with the lord of the land?" Joy said, with a bitterness that dismayed him.

"Nay, but neither do they offer themselves to me, a far more personal act, wouldn't you say?"

She flushed and frowned. "I have spent long years holding onto that which is mine against the encroachment of men, so you will pardon me if I was wary of trusting you at first sight. What if you were the kind who would send for Hobart?"

Campion shook his head, understanding her reluctance and yet smarting from it. "But now, surely, you must know I would do nothing to hurt you."

She laughed at his words, an unhappy sound that made Campion flinch. Had he hurt her? How? Surely not with his rebuffs? "Joy, I was trying to do what was best for you."

Her chin lifted, and her violet eyes flashed. "And how could you be certain what is right for me? You may have ruled wisely and well for a lifetime, but you are not omnipotent, my lord. You cannot possibly know everything!"

Campion stilled, astounded, not for the first time, by her perception. She was right, of course. Years of making decisions, of running his demesne, of arbitrating over the disputes of his people and taking care of his family had left him all too accustomed to proffering answers whenever questions were presented to him. Had he become pompous and imperious?

Campion made a low sound of apology as the realization struck him that this time, perhaps, he had been wrong. He reached out to take her hand, to tell her so, but all the fine arguments he had prepared vanished in a swell of foreboding.

"Marry me," he said, the words coming hurriedly as emotions buffeted him. He needed time to think upon her words, to take a good, long look at himself, yet his blood was beating out a demand that he do something now, before it was too late.

But it was already too late. As Joy shook her head in denial, Campion knew he had rejected her once too often, sealing his fate, along with her own. She pulled her hand from his and stood, as if to dismiss him.

Lifting her chin in that familiar gesture of defiance, she faced him, and Campion could see that her anger was barely controlled. "I want no proposal born of pity," she said. "I have already suffered one marriage arranged for reasons other than affection, and I will not be a party to another, thank you."

"'Tis not an offer born of pity, nor one I make lightly," Campion said. But she shook her head, backing toward the door, and he felt the situation slipping away from him. For the first time in years beyond count, he was not in control.

"And what of your uncle?" he asked, desperate to stay her.

"I'll evade him. It's a game we play and not your concern." The look of contempt she gave him made him surge to his feet.

"And what about your feelings for me? Are they so easily forgotten? What of that which you asked of me? Were you going to share my bed and then leave, without so much as a word?" Campion asked, risking his pride with the question.

Joy's eyes widened and her expression was stricken, but she nodded. And before he could respond, she hurried through the doorway, as if she could no longer bear his presence.

Her answer so shocked him that Campion made no move to follow. Instead, he sank down upon the stool in unaccustomed confusion, mind and body in a turmoil such as he had little known in his life. Anger and hurt and disbelief all warred together as he stared after her, unwilling to accept what had just occurred. He had ruled his demesne long and well, there being little over the years that was beyond the reach of his will.

It was a humbling experience to be so thoroughly thwarted, and yet Campion's thoughts were on the loss of what might have been. He had given a life to his king, his lands, his people, and his sons, yet now... *What of me?* he thought in the stillness of the solar. *What of my joy?*

The Earl of Campion could not remember ever being so uncertain. Deeming it best to let the passions that had flared in the solar cool before he spoke again with Joy, he had retired to his chamber, where he hoped to bring his jumbled thoughts and emotions to order. But when one of the villeins reported a block of ice had broken off, threatening to dam the river, he was glad for a chance to go out and tackle a task with which he was well familiar.

He would speak again with Joy when he was finished. Meanwhile, he took pleasure in riding his favorite destrier and directing the movements of the men who were breaking up the frozen water. He even got down and lent a hand, despite Reynold's protests, for if his son could aid them without complaining about his bad leg, then Campion could work, too.

He was wet and cold and feeling his age when at last they returned to the castle, his thoughts firmly fixed upon a hot bath. It was only after he was clean and dry and fortified by a hot cup that his thoughts turned once more toward Joy.

Obviously, Stephen was wrong, and Joy was not after his money, else she would have agreed to marry him eagerly. Why, then, had she pursued him so diligently? No matter what her bold speech, Campion sensed that she was not a woman to make free with her favors. She had too much of the air of innocence about her for that.

Then, why? Campion could come up with only one conclusion. Joy truly had wanted him and cared for him. The knowledge settled like a warm ember around his heart, firing his blood and rousing him to action. Surely, all the disagreements between them could be resolved somehow, for didn't he return that regard?

No, he thought ruefully. Regard was too mild a name for what he felt for Joy, and he was determined to tell her so, to persuade her by any means possible that she belonged here, by his side. And with new resolve he went below to look for her.

Down in the hall he found Stephen still at the high table, for he had not gone to the river, dismissing the need with a clever remark. It appeared that the boy was still sulking. As Joy must be, Campion decided, for she was not among the revelers, nor in the solar. "Have you seen Lady Warwick?" he asked.

"She's gone," Stephen said.

"Gone?" Campion echoed, uncertain he had heard his son correctly.

"She left before the meal, soon after you went out to break up the ice."

Joy was gone? Campion ignored the rapid pounding of his heart as he tried to make sense of his son's speech. "But where did she go?"

Stephen shrugged carelessly. "I know not. Perhaps back home to face her uncle or on to another demesne to work her wiles on a new lord."

Campion stiffened. "You mean, she has packed her things and taken to the roads, with her train?" At Stephen's nod, the earl leaned forward, palms spread upon the table in an effort to control the emotions that swept through him. "Why didn't you send word to me?"

Stephen shrugged again. "I knew not where you were along the river or that you would even care to be notified. And far be it from me to involve myself in the affairs of a lady who warned me well to stay out of her business," he added, with a sneer.

"But why? Why would she leave so suddenly?" Campion asked in astonishment, throwing up his hands. Joy was a strong woman, not the sort to cringe and sneak away like a thief in the night. What had driven her to flee?

"She probably didn't like being found out," Stephen drawled.

His son's taunt drew Campion up short, and he leaned upon the table once more. Staring long and hard at the son who so sorely tried his patience, he realized that it was time he spoke. "Aren't you too old to sulk like a boy just because a pretty woman doesn't fancy you?" he asked.

Stephen's head came up swiftly, his eyes glittering. "And aren't you too old to be chasing after a skirt?"

A long moment of silence passed until Campion finally spoke. “No. I am no doddering invalid. I am a man. What of you, Stephen? What do you call yourself?”

At the question, Campion saw his son’s hand tighten around the ever present cup of wine until the knuckles grew white. Then, without a word, Stephen knocked it aside and swung to his feet. He stalked away, leaving Campion alone at the high table with Reynold, who watched Stephen go with a somber expression.

“He is smarting because you bested him for the lady’s affections when he is proud of his way with women. ’Tis all he has,” Reynold said.

“No. You’re wrong,” Campion said, as he, too, stared after his errant son. “’Tis not all he has, but ’tis a pity he thinks so.” Although it pained him, Campion knew that nothing could be done until Stephen decided for himself that he was more than a careless charmer.

With a sigh, Campion swung his gaze toward the window. Outside, the sky was clear, but the shadows were lengthening. Although the snow had begun to melt with the recent warmth, the roads would still be half frozen and muddy and difficult. Was she all right? The knowledge of her departure returned to him with the force of a blow.

Joy was gone.

And for all Campion’s wealth and power, there was nothing he could do about it. As his guest, she was free to leave when she will, and he had to accept her decision. But she had come into his life like a force of nature, stirring up his safe and staid existence until he felt so good that he wanted to reach out and grasp life in his hands. *And he didn’t want to let go.*

Campion had thought to make her see reason, to talk her into taking him as her husband, but wisdom and reason were what had made him refuse her in the first place. They were no use to him. Nor were all his vows to honor and protect a lady in distress. He saw them now for what they were: convenient excuses to have what he wanted without any of the attendant guilt.

To have *Joy*. And now that she was gone, Campion saw too well his mistake. He had been thinking with his mind, patiently deliberating when he ought to have listened to the heart that had wakened in his chest and the desire that thundered through his body. Joy was a fire in his blood, and now it ran cold with the want of her. How long ago had she left? he wondered as he whirled around.

Reynold met his panicked gaze and spoke haltingly. "Mayhap she wanted to be married for her own sake, not any other reason," he said, and the stark look in his eyes made Campion pause. Reynold disdained romantic love, and yet, his words held a yearning for someone to see beyond the limp that loomed so large in his own mind.

Just as Campion should have seen beyond his own image of himself as too mature and dignified to succumb to the charms of a beautiful young woman. Dignity be damned! It was time he admitted that he lusted after Joy in a shockingly primitive manner. And he not only admired her, but loved her with a strength the like of which he had never known before.

But he had pushed her away. Would she believe him now when he admitted his feelings? Shoving aside the doubts of his mind, Campion seized upon the determination of his heart. It was time for action. He strode for the door, calling for his sword and his steed.

"Where are you going?" he heard Reynold ask.

"I'm going after her!" Campion shouted over his shoulder. And he was coming back with her, too, he decided, a smile beginning to curve his lips. It had been a long time since life had thrown him a challenge, and now he found himself taking up the gauntlet with relish.

For Joy.

Campion flung open the doors to his great hall with a stubborn willfulness that even the woman squirming in his arms could not match. He had found her still upon his lands and, without stopping to argue, he had lifted Joy from her horse to his own. When they reached the entrance to the hall, she had balked, and so Campion had simply thrown her over his shoulder.

"Campion! Have you lost your senses?" she cried from behind him, but he dismissed her shouts and the pummeling of her small fists against his back with a grunt of enjoyment. He felt more alive than he had in years. He barely noticed the cheers from the servants, whether delighted at his retrieval of Joy or anticipating the First Foot of the new year as a harbinger of good luck to come.

Campion needed no such omen. He knew that his life had taken a turn that would provide him with joy aplenty, for he held it in his arms. And despite his wiggling burden, he climbed up the stairs with an effortless stride to stalk straight into the great chamber.

He suspected that he ought to kick the door shut, but that seemed a little violent for his taste, so he carried his prize to the bed, tossing her onto the wide expanse before returning to close and bolt the heavy oak entrance. When he faced her once more, Campion smiled at the sight of Joy, here in his room, alone with him. Since the night of her arrival, he had pictured her in his bed, and he knew a soul-stirring satisfaction to finally have her there.

She was a tangle of cloak and skirts, her mass of heavy black curls falling over her shoulders to her waist, and the earl had a tantalizing glimpse of one slender ankle. As he watched in silence, she struggled up on her knees and lifted those small pale hands to push back her unruly mane. Campion stiffened at the thought of those delicate fingers running through his hair, touching his body. *Soon.* He felt an exhilaration such as he had never known before, as if she alone had tapped some wildness he had long held in check.

"What are you doing?" she demanded, and Campion girded his loins for a pitched battle.

"I'm taking the matter out of your hands," he said, smiling at his own words.

Her mouth formed an O of astonishment that made him feel absurdly pleased before she managed to recover her usual poise. "See here, Campion, if this primitive display is fueled by some misguided sense of honor—"

Campion felt his grin widen, and he reached down to unclasp his sword. "Oh, I guarantee you that honor has nothing to do with it."

His gaze never left her as he dropped the weapon and moved forward, and he thoroughly enjoyed the shocked expression that came over her face. Joy had always been the aggressor, trying his control with her guileless attempts at seduction, but now it was his turn, and when he kicked off his boots and approached the bed with deliberate purpose, her violet eyes widened in surprise.

He reached her and lifted his hand to test one long, dark lock between his fingers, while delighting in Joy's speechless, breathless stare. "I'm afraid you were under a mistaken impression when you left here in such a cowardly manner," he said.

The words made her lift her chin, as he intended, and her eyes flashed. "Cowardly? I—"

"Don't ever run from me again," Campion said. It was not a threat or a plea, only a statement of fact, but, being Joy, she opened her mouth to argue. He didn't let her, distracting her with his movements as he leaned over her to slip her cloak off and away.

"Because you are mine, Joy," he said, answering any unspoken questions. "*My Joy.* Whether you will it or not. You started this between us, and now I've a mind to finish it," he said, his voice a low rumble as he lowered his mouth to take hers, *to make her his wife.*

She tasted as rich and ardent as he remembered, more so, in fact, for this time they were both unfettered by restraint. He pressed her back into his bed, losing himself in the pleasure of her kisses, his hands in the thick heaviness of her hair, his body in the soft embrace of hers.

He had been right about Joy's passionate nature, for she

soon displayed her eagerness, fumbling delightfully as she tried to remove his tunic and stroking his chest in wonder, just as if she had never touched a man before. Her guileless movements excited him beyond measure, and Campion, too, felt as if all were new to him.

Although he had loved both his wives, he recalled his nights with them with a warmth that little resembled this frantic heat. Joy was bold in her demands, pulling at his clothes, stroking his skin, and rubbing her breasts against his chest, as she moaned in a manner that ignited his desires. He could not get enough of her and nearly tore her gown in his haste to have her naked beneath him.

Just a few days ago, Campion might have been horrified by his actions, but his blood was running too fierce to hesitate. Joy was not satisfied with tender caresses, and suddenly, he wasn't either. She had unleashed something inside him that made him mad for her, a certain madness that would not be eased by sweet kisses and light touches, but that craved a deeper, unbridled union.

In the throes of this blessed madness, Campion kissed her throat, her breasts, and her stomach, while his hands roved over her smooth skin, exploring every curve and hollow. When at last he nudged her thighs open, Joy cried out in welcome. And when he cupped her there, he felt her teeth rasp against his shoulder in response.

Campion groaned, seizing her hips in his grasp, his fear of hurting her the only thing that kept him from taking her with a wildness he had never imagined. But as he waited, poised above her, his body shuddering with the force of his restraint, he realized that Joy was no gentle virgin, but a widow. Relief swamped him, and with a lusty cry, Campion drove himself into her body.

Too late, he felt the give of her maiden's barrier and her jerk of pain, for he was already buried deep inside her. Shocked, he lifted his head to look down at her flushed face. "Joy?" he whispered.

She gazed up at him, her violet eyes wide, but holding no rebuke. "I suppose now would be as good a time as any to tell you that my marriage was never consummated."

With a groan, Campion rested his forehead against hers, trying to think of something to say to sooth her, to apologize, but his usual eloquence deserted him, for the rest of his body clamored for something other than words. And then he heard the soft sound of her laugh.

He lifted his head once more. "Forgive me," he murmured, just as she said the same, and Campion felt his own rumble of laughter, a robust release that made him marvel at lovemaking where humor and ardor could exist together. Joy might be the virgin, but he felt as if she were teaching him afresh. And there was still so much to share with her, he realized, as his body suddenly reminded him of its position inside her own.

He kissed her hair and her ear and her throat, reveling in the taste of her salty skin, while she made soft sounds of delight, her laughter fading away when he rolled onto his back, so that she rested along his length. "Better?" he whispered.

"What?" She lifted her head, an expression of disbelief on her delicate features. "I shall die if it gets any better," she answered breathlessly. And suddenly all amusement left him as he moved, joining her in that sentiment. His efforts to go slowly were hampered by her impatient movements and her soft sounds of encouragement. Finally, he lost all control, giving himself up to his joy until her husky cry brought on his own shout of pleasure.

In the relative quiet of the aftermath, she rested upon him, her slight weight negligible, and Campion held her close as exhaustion claimed him. His new bride would either be the death of him or revitalize him beyond his wildest dreams, he thought, his lips quirking.

"There is something else I forgot to tell you," she murmured, and Campion stiffened as she lifted her face to meet his gaze, her black hair an inky curtain around them. What now? he wondered, with no little alarm. But then she gave him a shy smile endearingly at odds with her former wantonness. "I love you."

Campion sucked in a breath as the strength of his own feelings threatened to overwhelm him. "And I love you, as I have never loved before."

Joy's violet eyes were wide and soft, and she leaned to press a kiss upon his mouth. When she pulled back, however, she tipped up her chin, and Campion nearly groaned at the sight that surely boded ill for him.

"I must say that as much as I enjoyed your rather barbaric efforts to win me, don't think that I'll stand for such tactics very often," she warned.

Campion frowned. "You'll marry me, Joy," he said, using his most regal tone.

"Yes," she murmured.

"Good," he said, sighing with relief. "Then there won't be any more primitive displays."

"Except in the bedchamber," Joy said, with a sly smile that roused his blood once more. Campion groaned.

"And there is one more thing," she said. Her dainty fingers played with the hair on his chest in a way that made it difficult to concentrate on her words. "You might have guessed that the rumors about my being barren are a little premature."

Startled from his contemplation of the feelings she was inducing in his body, Campion lifted his head and laughed aloud. Everything about Joy was a joy, he thought, his arms tightening around her.

"I hope you are not set against more children, just in case," she said, a hint of vulnerability showing in her violet eyes.

"Oh, I would welcome more babies," Campion said, in all truth. He knew a sudden exhilaration at the notion and laughed again. "But is the world ready for more de Burghs?"

EPILOGUE

New Year's Day dawned clear and shiny as a piece of silver, just as if the Earl of Campion himself had decreed it, and Joy wondered for a moment if the man had dominion over the weather itself, causing it to strand her here to serve his purpose. The thought was not quite as improbable as it might seem, for had he not won dominion over her, a feat seemingly as impossible as ordering the snow and ice?

Yet as she stood in the great hall, watching the preparations for the feast to follow her wedding, Joy could not summon any regrets. Roesia had been right. There was no stopping love, and she would sacrifice all for it. Yet she sacrificed nothing in marrying Campion, who would not be a master, but a partner.

The future that had so often seemed bleak and difficult looked bright as a new coin, full of the promise of sharing a life with this wonderful man and even the possibility of children of her own, a dream she had long ago dismissed.

But even if that did not happen, she was part of a family. And what a family it was! Around her the hall was humming with the congratulations of the servants, genuinely happy at the news of the betrothal. Even Stephen seemed resigned, if not enthused about the marriage.

"I suppose there's no help for it," he had said with a shrug, lifting his cup in salute. "But I refuse to call you mother."

Joy had laughed, her heart too full to care as she waited for the priest and the guests to arrive. Although word had gone out, inviting all within Campion's lands to attend, none had yet entered the hall, as if they were awaiting some sign. When Joy had asked why, Wilda informed her that none dared to be the First Foot of New Year's Day.

Apparently, the first person over the threshold was responsible for the whole year in some way that Joy did not fully comprehend. And since she and Campion had arrived before midnight, all were watching the doors for the first official entrant.

Just as Joy grew impatient with such nonsense, there was a great commotion outside, as if the approach of many horses, while someone shouted about a party at the gate. Wedding guests? Remembering her own unforeseen appearance, Joy did not know what to expect, and she found herself watching nearly as breathlessly as Wilda. Although she cared little enough for superstition, this was her home now, and all who entered here would affect her.

A hush fell over the hall while each servant stopped to look, and then the great doors were flung open, and in strode a huge knight, followed by several others, and Joy knew a moment's fright. Frozen in place, she watched him doff his helm and shake out his dark hair—oddly familiar dark hair—and then a cheer rose up around her as all greeted the man's appearance as a good omen of the year to come.

And then Campion was hurrying forward to embrace the massive creature amid the cries of his people. "My lord Wessex!" they shouted. Was this Campion's eldest son, Dunstan? But even as Joy tried to identify the man, she was surrounded by others until she felt buffeted by a sea of humanity: tall, dark-haired men, ladies in elegant costume, squalling infants, servants and outriders, all talking excitedly while the dogs barked their own loud greetings. It was an impossible din, and yet Joy could not help smiling.

It was Campion's family, and never had she seen such a happy reunion. She tried to hang back amid all the poignant welcomes, but to her astonishment, she, too, was embraced, by a petite, brown-haired lady.

"Hello! I'm Marion, Dunstan's wife," she said, smiling the most beautiful smile Joy had ever seen, complete with two dimples. Joy smiled back, uncertain how to respond until she felt a familiar arm pull her close and the solid warmth of Campion's body.

She leaned against it, no longer deeming herself weak for

taking the comfort he offered, for this family was a bit overwhelming, in size, clamor, and sheer physicality. Joy would have felt dwarfed by them all, but for Marion, who, despite her stature, seemed as impressive as the rest of them.

And then, just as suddenly as it had started, the noise faded away to low murmurs, and all eyes turned toward Campion. How did he gain their attention so easily? Joy wondered, with pride and just a touch of awe. He smiled, and Joy could see just how much he was affected by the presence of these people.

"Welcome, my sons, but why would you brave such weather?" he asked.

"We were all at Wessex!" someone answered.

"Aye. They've been there for weeks, eating up my stores," the big one, called Dunstan, grumbled. "But we were loath to travel the last miles to Campion until the snow stopped."

Campion laughed with pleasure. "Then I shall not scold you for your trip, but welcome you gladly. You're just in time for the wedding!"

"A wedding! You haven't even met my wife yet!" a tall, somewhat grim fellow groused, seemingly annoyed at being upstaged. "Who is it? I suppose it's you!" he said, glaring at Stephen, as if the two had long been at odds.

Stephen made a low sound of disgust. "'Tis not me, nor will it ever be me, for I have more sense than the rest of you."

All the dark heads surrounding them swiveled toward Reynold. "Don't look at me," he said, with a grunt.

"Who then?" Dunstan growled.

Reynold tilted his head toward their father.

"Father?" Dunstan stared at his sire with such an expression of astonishment that Joy nearly laughed.

"Oh, how wonderful!" Marion rushed forward to embrace him and then hugged Joy once more. "I knew you were someone special," she whispered.

Joy was grateful for the welcome and the support implicit when Marion moved to stand beside her, for she faced seven strapping knights, two rather ferocious looking females, and a number of attendants, holding at least two babies. She swallowed, feeling distinctly uncomfortable under their regard, and she lifted her chin.

"This is Joy, soon to be Lady Campion," the earl said, and the glance he sent her was so filled with pride and love that Joy's anxiety eased. "At first she refused to marry me, but I finally managed to convince her, so please make her welcome, as I don't want to chase off after her again to bring her home."

Low laughter filled the hall, and Joy heard a voice call out, "Sounds like he got himself a stubborn wench!"

Although her face flamed, she could not help but smile when three of the knights turned a sympathetic expression toward their father. The grim one was heard to mutter, "Then he joins the rest of us."

Joy laughed aloud when a beautiful blonde beside him elbowed him in the ribs so hard that he grunted. Then the woman stepped forward, and suddenly Joy was surrounded not by dark knights, but by lovely ladies.

"Ignore them," said a slender, ginger-haired woman, directing a fierce frown toward the de Burghs.

"Yes! You are the one who has our sympathy," the blond one said. "I'm Bethia, and I know 'tis not every woman who can handle the men of this family."

"Well, I did not want to give up my independence," Joy said, seeking to explain the reluctance Campion had mentioned. And to her surprise all three of the women nodded in agreement.

"Neither did we," Bethia said.

Joy blinked in confusion. "Then why did you wed?"

All three women glanced at each other before eyeing Joy with what could only be called wicked grins. Then Bethia leaned close, with a meaningful nod toward the men who stood not far away. "'Tis obvious enough," she said.

"As I'm sure you've discovered, these de Burghs can be most persuasive!"

ABOUT THE AUTHOR

Deborah Simmons began her writing career as a journalist, but left non-fiction for the world of happily ever afters. She's the author of twenty-eight novels and novellas originally published by Avon, Harlequin, and Berkley, as well as an indie romantic comedy.

Her books *A Lady of Distinction* and *The Gentleman Thief* were finalists for Romance Writers of America's annual RITA competition. And two other releases, *The Gentleman's Quest* and *Glory the Rake*, were up for The Daphne du Maurier Award of Excellence for Mystery/Suspense. Her work has been translated and published in more than thirty countries, with graphic novel editions available in Japanese.

DeborahSimmons.com
Facebook.com/authorDeborahSimmons

WORKS BY DEBORAH SIMMONS:

A Heart's Masquerade
Fortune Hunter
Silent Heart
The Squire's Daughter
The Devil's Lady
The Vicar's Daughter
Taming the Wolf
The Devil Earl
Maiden Bride
Tempting Kate
A Wish for Noel
The de Burgh Bride
The Last Rogue
Robber Bride
The Unexpected Guest
The Gentleman Thief
My Lord de Burgh
The Companion
The Bachelor Knight
My Lady de Burgh
The Notorious Duke
A Man of Many Talents
A Lady of Distinction
The Dark Viscount
Reynold de Burgh: The Dark Knight
The Gentleman's Quest
Glory and the Rake
The Last de Burgh
It Had to Be You

www.ingramcontent.com/pod-product-compliance
Lightning Source LLC
Chambersburg PA
CBHW051313170626
46809CB00004B/1884